# JUST
# STEEL

# ALSO BY ED ORSZULA

*One More Time*

# JUST STEEL

**A Justin Steel Mystery/Thriller**

**by**

# Ed Orszula

**A Chris Mystery Book**

**Harvard**

First Edition

The characters and events in this book are fictitious. Any similarities
to real persons, living or dead, are coincidental and not intended by
the author.

ISBN:0-9701596-0-9

Library of Congress Catalog Card Number: 00-91985


Chris Mystery Books
Chris Mystery Publishing
P.O. Box 471
Harvard, Illinois  60033




Printed in the United States

*This book is dedicated to my children
and my grandchildren . . .
who will be here long after this book
is forgotten.
. . . They are my true legacy.*

## Acknowledgment

*Special thanks to Larry Starzec
for his guidance, support,
and friendship.*

# JUST
# STEEL

# Chapter 1

Outside, the arctic wind ushered in a white blinding snow, typical for the Chicago area in early December. Red Bud street was deserted. A bulb in the corner light post flickered in the driving white frenzy. Inside the elegant Tudor, there was a contrasting hue of frenzy. The color was red, the red of blood, and the red was everywhere. And in particular, the blood was on the ten inch hunting knife, and on the hands that held it, the hands of nineteen year old Brad Kendall.

Sabina Rockwald and Brad Kendall had dated for the last two years. She was now a senior in high school and he was a college freshman. They were a cute couple, a contrast in size and shape. He outweighed her by at least a hundred pounds and was a full head taller.

Sabina, or Sibby, as everyone called her, and Brad were inseparable during those two years. They attended the Glen-Deer High School dances together, the Homecoming, the Winter Hop, the Prom. He watched her run track and play basketball at the prestigious high school situated on Lake Michigan in affluent Northern Cook County. In turn, she attended his football, basketball, and baseball games.

It was in football that Brad Kendall excelled, garnering first team all conference honors as an offensive guard and second team for Northern Cook County. Several Division II colleges around the country offered him full 14athletic scholarships and Minnesota of the Big Ten expressed interest but Brad did not want to be apart from his Sibby. He turned them all down, much to his parent's dismay. They compromised by Brad enrolling at the University of Chicago as an off-campus full-time student. As a Division III school, they had a football team, but could not offer an athletic scholarship.

Commuting from the north side to the south side was time consuming and required a reliable automobile, which his father provided. During football season, it seemed that all he did was get home, go to sleep, and get up to do it all over again the next day. Some nights, he was so worn out that he crashed with one of his teammates by sleeping on the floor in their room. It was safer and smarter than driving tired. The football coach would have preferred that Brad live on campus, but he was glad to accept him and his football talents under any circumstances.

Though Brad's parents chose to live in fashionable Glen-Deer, it took every cent that his father earned. The tuition demands at the University of Chicago were catastrophic to a family just making ends meet, but with grants, loans, and Brad agreeing to work part-time when he wasn't playing football, they structured a plan that his parents could handle.

In high school, Brad had been an A student and at the University of Chicago he was managing a B minus in the first semester. This was a fine achievement because the University of Chicago was a very demanding institution. Taking football, working part-time, and traveling to school each day into consideration, it was remarkable what he accomplished.

But it was all worth it because he could be close to Sibby.

Only moments ago, Brad Kendall had removed the knife from the chest of forty-one year old Richard Rockwald. Blood spurted all over Brad's face, chest, arms, and hands in the process. He stood stunned, and for what seemed an eternity to him, he gaped at the bound and gagged, mutilated body of Sibby's father.

"My father doesn't think we should see each other anymore," said Sibby.

Brad was floored. "Why?" he asked.

"He wants me to attend St. Marisa College in the east, like my mother."

"Tell him, no," said Brad.

"I already told him I would go," said Sibby.

"I thought we wanted to stay together," he pleaded.

"No, you wanted us to stay together," she said, her head down.

15

"I figured we were getting married when I finished college. We need to be close," he said.

"I like you. I like you a lot," she said. "But we have to grow up. I think going away is a good idea. It's too early to talk about marriage. We can still date each other. But I really think we should date others, too."

She handed his high school ring back to him. He took it, closed his fist on it, and closed his eyes so she wouldn't see the tears welling up.

"Your father put you up to this, didn't he?" spurted Brad.

"Both my parents agreed," she said, calmly.

"Why are they turning you against me?" pleaded Brad.

"It's not like that, Brad. They only want what's best for me," she said.

"And I'm not the best," his voice trailed off.

"You're twisting it," she said.

His face revealed the anger inside of him. "Your parents are arrogant, stuck-up, sons-of-bitches, and now you've become just like them," he said.

"That's a terrible thing to say," she replied. She looked at the blood that appeared between his fingers as he squeezed the ring she had returned to him.

"To hell with your parents and to hell with you," he shouted.

"I don't think we should see each other anymore," she said.

"All that I've done for you and all that we've meant to each other and now you kick me in the balls."

"Please don't phone me anymore," she said. He was beginning to frighten her.

"I'll see you and your fucking family dead," he said with his teeth clenched.

Not believing what she had heard, she covered her ears with her hands as if they would stop the barrage of hatred he spewed at her. She slapped his face and regretting her own violence, brought her hand to her mouth. Sobbing, she turned and ran home.

With his left hand, Brad took the ring from his bloody right hand and placed it in his shirt pocket. With surprise, he looked at the blood in his aching right hand, then wiped it on his jeans.

Brad Kendall began to realize the gravity of the words he said and feared he could not take them back. Sibby had hurt him suddenly and deeply. He tried to defend himself from her words by trying to ward them off with words of his own. He had never spoken that way to her before, never had to. He scared himself at how angry he had become. On the football field, he forced himself to roll over his opponents. But this was different. This was an anger from somewhere way inside of him, an anger that he wished he had not summoned up.

The next week was the Thanksgiving holiday and each day Brad called Sibby but she refused to speak to him. When Mrs. Rockwald answered the phone, she politely asked him not to bother her daughter. When Mr. Rockwald answered, he threatened Brad with arrest and legal action. Sibby was there when he called, but she ignored his pleas.

Rage grew inside Brad Kendall.

In the deathbed, next to the body of Richard Rockwald was Donna Rockwald, his thirty-nine year old wife. Her mouth was frozen with an expression of terror and agony. Nearly forty stab wounds had penetrated her body, which now rested in a pool of drying blood. The foes of Brad Kendall had been vanquished. He stared in silent horror and disbelief at the carnage before him.

"I know you've been sleeping with my wife," said an angry Frank Rockwald, thirty-seven year old brother of Richard. "I just haven't figured out how long it's been going on."

"I don't know what you're talking about," said a coy Richard.

"Don't deny it," said Frank. "Kathy told me everything. She told me how you wouldn't let her break it off. Well, it's over now."

"Don't make such a big deal out of it," said a non-contrite Richard. "Kathy couldn't get from you what she needed, so I gave it to her."

"Get out of my house before I kill you," said the younger brother.

"You don't have the balls for it, little brother," needled Richard.

Frank Rockwald vowed to himself that he would one day kill his brother.

"Mr. Rockwald, this is Brad Kendall. I would like to come over to talk to you about Sibby."

"Don't bother," said Richard Rockwald..

"Please sir. It's very important to me," said Brad.

"It's not important to me," said Rockwald.

"I'm coming over now," said a determined Brad, "and you can't stop me."

"You show up here, creep, and I'll break you like a pretzel," said Rockwald.

Frustrated and crazy with anger, Brad slammed down the receiver. Instead of going to the Rockwald house, he

18

bought a twelve pack of Old Style and sat in his car in his garage and drank until he couldn't remember anymore.

"Who was that on the phone, Daddy?" asked Sibby.

"That was Brad, the nerd, threatening to come here."

"I'm sorry for all the trouble, Daddy."

"That's all right, pumpkin. He just has a hard head and doesn't have enough sense to know when he's not wanted."

"I'm going now, Daddy."

"Where to?"

"The library."

"Don't stay out too late."

"The library closes at nine. I'll be home right after," she sang out.

"Which car are you taking?"

"I'm not. Maggie is picking me up." Maggie was her best friend.

"Be careful."

"Yes, Daddy."

With the knife still in his hands, Brad Kendall surveyed the bodies of twelve year old Cindy Rockwald and fourteen year old Richie Rockwald as they peacefully laid in the beds in their respective rooms. Moments earlier they had been grotesquely and violently strangled by powerful hands. The senseless slaughter of unfulfilled lives was laid to waste. Brad Kendall rued the broken bodies before him and headed for the front door.

A subdued figure sat in the shadow of the poorly lit office. His arms were placed on the rests of the black leather easy chair. His legs were crossed at the knees. He leaned forward slowly, uncrossing his legs, tenting his hands beneath his chin, a pensive look on his tanned face. His black hair was combed sleekly back. He had eyes to match the color of his hair, but dull and without life. His manicured fingernails looked out of place on his rugged, weather-beaten hands. He spoke softly. "How much does Richard Rockwald owe us as of today?"

"Two point five mil," said the submissive second man standing before his boss.

"What was the original amount?" asked the boss.

"One point two mil"

"Any payment?" asked the boss.

"Zip," answered the man.

"Does he understand    the terms and the con-sequences?" asked the boss.

"He says he does."

"Has he been warned?" said the boss.

"Duly," said the standing figure.

"What was his response?" The boss perked his head a bit forward.

"He threatened to go to the cops."

The boss sat back in his chair and crossed his legs again. He shook his head in regret. "Bad investment," he said. "Do you agree?"

"I agree."

"Write him off," said the boss.

"Consider it done."

"Cover your tracks," said the boss.

"I always do."


Maggie dropped Sibby off at the curb in front of her house. They had  just returned from the library. Sibby

20

tried to get out of the car, weighted down by eight or nine heavy manuals and texts she had just checked out.

"Don't drop those books," laughed Maggie.

"Don't worry about me. You drive home safely. See you at school tomorrow," said Sibby.

Approaching the house and making fresh tracks in the newly fallen snow, she trudged up the front steps. Seeing no lights on in the house, she fumbled for her key. She attempted to unlock the front door with one hand as she balanced her books in her free hand. To her surprise, the door was slightly ajar. She cautiously pushed the door open with her foot and carefully entered the dark foyer.

A figure in the darkness startled her and she stepped back but reflexively clutched her books. When she looked again, she saw it was Brad Kendall, covered with blood and holding a bloody knife. Now as she dropped her books, he dropped the knife. He reached for her but she ducked under him. In the darkness, he sprawled over her into the fresh snow on the front porch, smearing some of his crimson stains into the innocent snow. Sibby only saw the contrasts of darkness and white.

"What have you done?" she screamed. "What have you done?"

"I'm sorry, Sibby," he pleaded. "I'm sorry."

As he reached for her, she frantically crawled away into the darkness of the front hallway, screaming, "get away from me, get away."

"I'm sorry, Sibby," he said one last time, as he turned and ran down the front steps, dropping red blood into the white snow. She stood up terrified and watched him run until he disappeared into a gust of snow and the darkness. She slammed the door and bolted it shut.

She turned her attention back to the house. Once she reached Cindy's room, she flicked on the light and saw her crumpled body. In a stupor, she went to Richie's room and found him the same way. In shock, as if she was in a bad dream from which she could not wake, one in which she tried to scream but nothing came out, she ran from room to room, in a daze, turning on lights.

Finally, managing a whimper, she mewed. "Mommy, Daddy, Cindy and Richie are dead. Help me! Help me!"

The last light she turned on was in her parent's bedroom. A feint scream entered her throat as she discovered their bodies, lifeless and bloody in their beds. Blood was everywhere. On the bed. On the walls, the ceiling, the floor, the night lamp. She reached out to touch them but pulled back, her hands covering her mouth.

"They're all dead. Oh my God. They're all dead." The scream in her throat tried to get out.

She went back to the front doorway, retracing her steps, trying to make sense, trying to make it go away. But she knew it was real when she saw her scattered books and the bloody knife on the floor. She turned the porch light on and saw Brad Kendall's bloody hand prints on the front door and finally let out her trapped scream. She ran through the front door, determined to find him. She flew down the stairs, raced into the street screaming, "son-of-a-bitch, son-of-a-bitch," until she too disappeared into the night.

Neighbor's porch lights came on sequentially following her screams in the snowy darkness. A distant police siren was heard.

Back at the house, an unseen intruder let himself out a window, and escaped to his waiting car. The hard falling snow rapidly obliterated his tracks.

# Chapter 2

Daytime in Chicago was not always safe. Nighttime was even less safe. There was a full moon in the sky on this summer night twelve years ago. As the moon slid behind a passing cloud and the alley darkened, two sinister silhouettes waited for just this moment to emerge from their hiding place.

Inside the brick bungalow, the Brisby family slept. It was a few minutes past midnight and the house was silent except for the air conditioners and the loud snores of Marshall Brisby, an accountant by day and a loving father always. Genevieve, his wife of nine years was next to him and snored softly. Their seven year old twins, Martin and Crispin, were silent in the bedroom adjoining theirs. They appeared content and calm, and probably dreamt about yesterday's picnic and pony rides.

Along with the kitchen, dining room, and parlor, the bedrooms were on the main floor. The dormered upper level was used exclusively for an extensive HO train layout that they all worked on since the twins were four. The basement was organized and neat. One corner held the washer and dryer; another highlighted the tool room. In the center was a regulation size Ping-Pong table. The rest of the area was dedicated to storage.

The glass falling from the breaking basement window was heard only by the slinking intruders. The opening in the window frame was just large enough for them to pass through.

Outside, the night was unusually cool for August. The air was dry. A mixture of freshly cut grass and the putrid smell of garbage cans produced an aroma of sour sweetness in contrast to the captured warm air from the afternoon and the basement's summer humidity. As they slithered through the opening and onto the concrete floor, the intruder's footsteps ground the broken glass like crunching hard candy.

Their flashlight beam preceded them up the wooden stairs to the main level. The door was unlocked.. The sounds of the two window air conditioners canceled their footfalls on the soft carpet as they initiated their search in the dining room.

Whether awakened by a premonition or by a need to urinate, Marshall Brisby, with only the plug-in night light in the kitchen to guide him, began his sleepy trek to the bathroom that was between the kitchen and the dining room. Had he remained asleep, the night might have ended differently. But he was awake and the flashlight beam was hard to miss.

The natural words from his mouth were, "who's there?" They were the only words he would utter as the flashlight crashed across his skull and removed his consciousness. He slumped to the floor with a thud.

The flashlight was in pieces on the floor, and the night light in the kitchen was only remotely visible, as the intruders panicked in the unfamiliar darkness. Mrs. Brisby woke up with a scream, flicked on the table lamp along side her bed, and was about to investigate the disturbance, when the sudden right fist of one of the invaders stopped her in her tracks. He used the other table lamp to crush in her head.

The twins hearing the ruckus called for Mommy when the second intruder snatched them.

Marshall Brisby started to come to and pleaded for the burglars not to hurt the boys. The dining room light was now on and it revealed a short Hispanic and a tall black.

"Didju fine da paperwork?" asked the Hispanic.

"Not enough time," said the black man.

"Wot we gonna do wid all dese people?" asked the Hispanic.

"We get rid of them. And if we can't find the paperwork, we make sure nobody else does," said the black man.

The black man held the twins with his left hand and Marshall Brisby with his right. Though Brisby struggled with all his might, the black man held him with relative ease.

The Hispanic went down to the basement and when he came back he held a can filled with gasoline and a switchblade. "You gonna die, Gringo," he said, laughing. Marshall saw the big scar under the Hispanic's chin. It

27

looked as if someone had once tried to slice his throat but miscalculated.

The switchblade and the gas can sent panic into Marshall Brisby. "No, please," he pleaded. "I'll give you whatever you want. Please don't hurt my family."

Both men laughed.

"Too late, Gringo," said the Hispanic. "You see our faces."

Marshall Brisby stood helpless as he watched the Hispanic slit the throats of the twins. It was over in two seconds. The black man held Brisby with his right arm around his neck and his left hand over his mouth. The thumb on his left hand was missing and Marshall Brisby saw this just before his mouth filled with vomit forcing the black man to withdraw his hand in disgust. The backhand swipe of the Hispanic's thrust aimed for the throat missed its mark and instead slashed across the right cheek of Marshall Brisby.

The black man threw Brisby to the floor and both men, now out of control, kicked him into unconsciousness again. He looked dead enough. With their anger released and their tempers subsided, both men went about the rest of their business.

When Marshall Brisby regained consciousness, every part of his body felt broken to him. He put his right hand to the warm wetness of his bleeding right cheek. He couldn't move his left arm. It was as if it wasn't there anymore. He started to cough and choke. Smoke and flames now came at him from every direction. He covered his nose and mouth with the handkerchief in his pajama pocket.

He remembered his wife and the twins and tried to get up but couldn't. He crawled toward them but the searing flames lashed at him and wouldn't allow him. He tried to crawl through the hot fire but when his pajamas ignited he rolled in pain attempting to extinguish himself.

Instinct instructed him to self-preservation and he somehow dragged himself with his one good arm to the front door. He seared his hand as he pulled himself up by the hot doorknob. Managing to open the door, he was in the doorway yelling for help when the explosion blew him away.

# Chapter 3

As his head jerked up from his pillow, he didn't know if he had hollered out or not. Instinctively he reached for the scar on his right cheek. It was still there. Marshall Brisby started each day with the same nightmare. It was five AM, his normal wake-up time.

After the tragic occurrence that took his family from him, he was mentally and physically incapacitated. His brother, who was a wealthy man, and who was still alive at the time, financed his recovery and provided the required nurture. The first year was the most difficult. Incentive to recover was lacking. Physically, for the most part his body healed. His broken ribs grew together again and had not punctured any organs. His left shoulder and arm were separated, dislocated and broken and though functional, would never be the same again. Plastic surgery on his cheek failed to completely conceal the wound and a three inch scar would be a reminder to him every time he looked in a mirror or touched his face.

Skin grafts on his back repaired burns from the fire and explosion. The skin on the palm of his right hand from the hot door knob, though later callused, would always exhibit tenderness.

His mental and psychological healing would take a lifetime and his first year was critical. He couldn't save his family because he was too weak. He blamed himself for their deaths. He felt guilt because he survived and they didn't. In depth and frequent psychiatric counseling sessions eventually lessened his despair. In time he realized that he must go on, that there had to have been a reason for his survival.

For that reason he became Justin Steel. As Marshall Brisby was weak, he wouldn't allow Steel to be so flawed. Though he could not save his family, he, as Justin Steel, had helped others in difficult situations, and would continue to do so as long as he was able. Only in this manner would he permit himself to live, in the service of others, in the name of his wife and children, and in the name of his brother, who shortly after he had rescued Marshall Brisby from himself, died in a commercial air crash. His will had set up a handsome trust for Brisby, now Steel, worth several million dollars. Steel never looked at the balance. He survived on the generous amount he received in the mail each month.

As an accountant in his previous existence, he had been studying to sit for his Certified Public Accountant's examination. He had long since stopped practicing accounting, much less considering taking the exam, but he still kept up with his reading on the changes in the accounting world. Many times, to his surprise, his knowledge of accounting and taxes had helped solve cases and address problems he encountered along the way in his new venue of helping the defenseless. He was now a licensed private investigator. He didn't advertise or even hang a shingle. He worked out of his home and his telephone was unlisted. He didn't want to be found easily. His licensure, however, made him legal.

His handsome monthly check provided him with financial freedom and the ability to choose his lifestyle. It didn't rid him of his mental demons. Neither did it make his life easy. Justin Steel didn't want his life to be easy as he embarked on his self inflicted arduous daily routine.

His hot shower cleansed his body and helped remove the remnants of his nightmare. He put on his well worn sweat suit and his sturdy running shoes in anticipation of his ten mile run in the McHenry County countryside.

Satisfied that the windows and the doors of the house were locked, he reset the alarm. It was still dark outside as he whistled, then hollered, "C'mon boy." His German Shepherd, Scrap Iron, responded. He unlocked the kennel gate and let the dog out. As he playfully jostled the dog, it affectionately licked his hands. This was actually the second Scrap Iron and was two years old. The first one was shot with a sniper's bullet that was intended for Steel. When the dog took the bullet, it was the first time Steel had cried since he lost his family. Steel later killed the sniper himself. The new dog took the old dog's place and soon won the heart of his master. But no mistake should be made; this dog was also a killer, and would respond to Justin Steel's command.

He sent the dog on its tour of the premises. While it systematically inspected and searched the ten acre estate, Steel had his morning glass of orange juice that he brought out with him, did some stretching exercises, and awaited the dog's return. First the dog circled the house then gradually fanned out toward the perimeter, letting its keen senses sniff out anything awry. Ten minutes later, the dog returned and was greeted with, "That's a good dog," and fresh water.

Patting the shoulder holster and .38 revolver under his sweat shirt, he and Scrap Iron set out on their run into the darkness. The October morning was a mixture of dew and early autumn frost. The air smelled fresh but damp. Steel wasted no time getting into his brisk run.

At forty-eight, Justin Steel had trained his body to compete with men half his age. And to be ready in case he should ever meet the Hispanic with the scar on his throat and the black man with the thumb missing on his left hand. He completed his ten mile run in about an hour and his circuitous route culminated at his front door. It was about six-thirty when he finished his cool down.

Many would have considered this an adequate workout, called it a day, and jumped in the shower. Justin Steel's regimen called for much more. Changing into a fresh, workout shirt and shorts, and a pair of cross-training shoes, not allowing his body to cool down, he headed for the weight room.

Six sets of squats on the Smith rack got him into the mood. Six more sets of ten reps each with 650 pounds of weight on the leg press machine finished his leg exercises. Back to the Smith rack for an equal amount of sets and reps, he benched 300 pounds, varying the width of his grip on the bar. Going from lat pull-downs to the rowing machine, he worked his upper and lower back. An assortment of biceps and triceps curls polished off his arms. Some parallel bar dips, ab crunches, and chin-ups added to his routine. Ten minutes on the light bag and another ten on the heavy bag finally did him in.

At six-two, he weighed 225 pounds. His chest measured forty-eight inches, his waist thirty-four inches, and his arms eighteen inches. He shopped at specialty stores to fit his body. Not too bad for a forty-eight year old former accountant. The sixty pounds he added since the loss of his family was all muscle. But he was never satisfied, constantly prodding his body to respond to his increased demands.

His more attractive physique wasn't a matter of vanity. His superior body strength and stamina had saved lives, his included, many times, over the last ten or so years. His mastery of Japanese karate, Korean tae kwon do, and kung-fu held him in good stead. If these failed him, he relied on his expertise with firearms.

All of these traits would have been useless if he had not sharpened his cunning and wit through the study of the criminal mind and the day to day experiences in the field. He drove himself to improve his intellect, his body, and his will. He could never be weak again.

With his workout over, he felt entitled to a long, relaxing shower. It was nine when he started to prepare his breakfast.  Dressed comfortably in jeans, tee shirt, and sandals, he ate heartily the meal of juice, natural cereal, two eggs, and black coffee. The rest of the day he would snack on fresh fruits and vegetables until it was time for dinner.

Some cases he worked on often lasted weeks or even months. He was in between clients, so he took full advantage of his seclusion to repair and prepare his body and mind. He caught up on stacks of newspapers and magazines that had accumulated. He further sharpened his mind with continuous study in all areas from astronomy to zymurgy. His day moved swiftly as he immersed himself in these endeavors.

About five in the evening, he treated himself to a steak, salad, and baked potato. Scrap Iron joined him for dinner and had two cans of Alpo and the steak bone. The dog was a good friend and a loyal companion, the only one Steel would allow to enter his life. By now, Steel was tired of reading and only watched television if something exceptional intrigued him. He allowed himself one glass of wine after dinner and some recorded music. He started out with CDs but invariably ended up with some old 45s or 33 LPs. It was when the old tunes played that the memories crashed in on him. He cried for the twins but mostly it was Genevieve, his wife, that he missed. He missed the companionship  no woman but his deceased wife could ever provide. If his thoughts became too painful he would go to the indoor shooting range in the basement of his house and fire off a few dozen rounds. Most times, he just went to bed early, alas, to dream.

# Chapter 4

He kept his home and phone under the name of
Marshall Brisby and usually the only calls he received
were from sales people and solicitors of various sorts.
Normally, the machine picked up and what calls he had
to return were infrequent. So when his private line rang,
the one dedicated to Justin Steel, it exhilarated him.
Those who had the number called only when it was
urgent or they needed help, and he disseminated his
number to only a few.

After several months of his tedious self-inflicted
schedule, he yearned to go out and do something useful.
Caught up with his reading, he was bored, especially with
his evenings, he needed action and diversion.

"Steel," he answered perfunctorily after the fourth
ring.

"Is this Justin Steel?" asked the man with a firm voice.

37

"Just Steel," said Justin Steel.

"Excuse me?" asked the puzzled caller.

"Just call me Steel." It was one of his idiosyncrasies that he preferred to be addressed in this manner and he was always very firm about it.

"Okay - Steel," said the man. "My name is Lester Rolland and I'm an Agent with the Federal Bureau of Investigation. You come highly recommended by Mike Collins of the Illinois State Bureau. He said you'd know his name and that we could talk."

"Talk," said Steel.

"Fine," said Rolland, a bit put off with the terse response. "What I'm about to share with you is sensitive and confidential. I've been told that you're someone who can be trusted and who is discreet."

"I can be and am," said Steel.

"Good," said Rolland, getting used to Steel's responses.

"Antiracketeering is how the Bureau enters the picture in this specific situation and I can't tell you everything but I can tell you what I think you need to know. About a month ago, a family was murdered in their home in Glen-Deer. Are you familiar with that occurrence?"

"Only what I've read in the newspaper," said Steel. "As I remember, the family's name was Rockwald and no one's been charged with the crime. You have no leads."

"That's not quite true," said Rolland. "We've kept some things from the press. The investigation of the murders is under local jurisdiction. They've asked for help from the Illinois Bureau. At the Federal level, we're crossing paths from a different direction. We're not working on the murders as much as on interstate

38

racketeering, something we were investigating before the murders occurred, something that may be connected, but we can't be sure. It could be a coincidental event."

"The whole family was killed?" injected Steel. "How horrible."

"Yes, it was," said Rolland, thinking to himself, finally, a human being at the other end of the line.

"What do you want from me?" asked Steel.

"We would like you to investigate the murders. The locals have run into a brick wall. They keep wanting to pin it on a kid on the run. His name is Brad Kendall. We'll give you family names, business connections, and any other leads we have. Your investigation may cross into ours and we'll expect your cooperation in that event."

"Fair enough," said Steel.

"There is a surviving daughter. The locals have been protecting her after the fact. My opinion is that if somebody wanted her dead, she'd be dead," said the FBI Agent.

"You're probably right," said Steel.

"Here's the deal. She'll be your client. You'll officially be working for her. She knows someone will be representing her but she doesn't know who. Your friend, Mike Collins, will introduce you to her. One more thing. She has no money. Her father was close to bankruptcy when he died. She can't pay you. Unofficially, we can cover your expenses, but that's the best we can do. Can you live with that?"

"I think so," said Steel.

"Mike said you would help. Thanks," said the FBI man.

"I'm not doing it for you," said Steel.

"Thanks, anyway," said Rolland. "By the way, it could be dangerous. I thought you should know."

"It often is," said Steel.

"I can have a package with more confidential information delivered to your home in an hour," said Rolland. "Will you be there?"

"I'll be here," said Steel.

"The Agent's name is Miller."

"Tell him to ring at the gate and I'll meet him there."


The package was the size of a storage box, the kind that holds a couple dozen files. Steel spent more than two hours reviewing its contents. He first looked at the stack of color eight-by-tens of the crime scene. The vividness of the atrocity struck at the very heart of him. The dead boy and girl reminded him of his deceased twin sons. When he studied the carnage of Richard and Donna Rockwald, he couldn't help thinking that the man could have and should have been himself beside his wife some twelve years ago. Once he saw the photos he knew he wouldn't quit until the guilty party or parties was apprehended and dealt with.

Setting the pictures aside, he read the files in the order they were in. The police report provided him with the facts he needed. He already knew the results. Death for all four had occurred on December fourth, approximately between seven and nine PM. The surviving daughter, Sabina Rockwald, left for the library shortly before seven and returned a little after nine. Excellent police work, scoffed Steel. After questioning her, the police ruled her out as a suspect. Burglars were suspected, but no clues led anywhere. It didn't have the markings of a professional killing since it was so brutal and chaotic. Only Brad Kendall's prints were found, on the doorway and on the knife he dropped in the girl's presence. He is their only suspect. He fled the scene and was still missing.

Steel next went to the file marked Brad Kendall. He was nineteen years old, an only child, and had been a freshman at the University of Chicago where he played football and earned good grades. His father, Kenneth Kendall, worked as an accountant for a medium-sized firm in downtown Chicago. Steel took a liking to him because of his occupation. The company provided janitorial services to companies in the Loop and the surrounding suburbs. His mother, Connie Kendall was a sales clerk in a bakery in nearby Glencoe. Brad lived at home, delivered pizzas part-time, and had never been in trouble before.

Sabina Rockwald's folder was next. It said she was a senior in high school but that she wouldn't graduate on schedule since she had missed several weeks of school. Had it not been for ten days of Christmas vacation, it would probably have been more, surmised Steel. *Poor kid,* thought Steel. *What a way to spend Christmas.* She was living with Frank Rockwald, her uncle, and his wife Kathy, in Skokie. He was the only sibling her dead father had. Her mother had an older sister, Miriam, who lived in Phoenix.

Sabina was seeing a psychiatrist, a Dr. Anita Hart. If anyone needed a shrink, surmised Steel, Sabina did. He could speak from first hand experience.

The rest of the box contained Richard Rockwald's business ventures. Besides the three pizza restaurants, he owned a grocery store, a bowling alley, and an import/export company. While there were a lot of papers, the details were sketchy at best.

Steel telephoned Mike Collins, his source at the Bureau and asked when he could meet his new client. Tomorrow at nine for breakfast at the IHOP in Skokie was agreed on. His suitcases were always packed in readiness so ten minutes to double check was all he needed. He decided to drive the gray Ford Taurus and quickly tucked the bags in the trunk. The car was fully serviced and the fuel tank was full. A quick check on his Smith & Wesson .38 and Colt .45 with plenty of ammunition were packed in a small leather attache' case. He wouldn't accidentally want to carry his weapons on board an aircraft if they were packed with his regular luggage. His passport was in order as was the rest of his identification. An array of credit cards under various company names were in his billfold. He was only going to Skokie and could very well be home tomorrow night but he learned long ago that it was better to be prepared for travel anywhere.

He phoned Gus and Emily Hessmuller and told them to come at seven tomorrow morning and he didn't know for how long this time. They cleaned his house and cared for the outside premises each Saturday but when he had to be away, they responded at a moment's notice. He paid them very well, better than they could do in any other endeavor. They were good people and trustworthy. In his absence they provided a presence in the home and cared for Scrap Iron. The dog, in turn, was obedient and affectionate toward them. What they didn't know is that if something were to happen to Steel, everything would be theirs, the house, the land, the dog, and a monthly allotment. But, in fact, they knew nothing about Justin

Steel. To them, he was Marshall Brisby. And when he was away from home, the Steel telephone line shut down, and only the Brisby telephone continued to function.

Justin Steel was anxious for tomorrow.

# Chapter 5

After Steel and Scrap Iron had their morning run, Steel instructed the dog to take care of Gus and Emily Hessmuller. In response, the dog licked his hands. Steel shaved and showered, sipped his coffee, and chose to skip his regular breakfast, as he waited for the caretakers to arrive.

The Hessmullers respected Justin Steel's guidelines about caution, though they didn't completely understand why. It couldn't be known when and if an enemy of Steel's would seek retribution. Anyone could be found regardless what precautions were taken, and Steel's abode was no exception. As instructed, the Hessmullers kept the gates and doors locked and admitted no one. They knew how to operate the alarm system and, if needed, the police were a phone call away. They also had Scrap Iron. The Hessmullers and the dog were comfortable with and were familiar with each other's routine.

Steel waved as he drove away on this cold January morning. It was below zero and a hint of light started to appear in the eastern sky. It looked to become a clear and crisp day but he knew it would soon snow. His left arm, a remnant of his injuries from twelve years ago, served as his personal barometer.

Out of his driveway, he turned right on McGuire Road and proceeded east to Alden Road, which he took north to Route 173, and went east. Though there were no expressways from Harvard, he still averaged fifty miles per hour for the forty mile trek to the I 94 toll road. He drove south to the Dempster Street exit and again headed east until he reached Skokie and the International House of Pancakes to meet with Mike Collins and Sabina Rockwald.

During his ride, he thought of how good it felt to be out again, as he savored the drive and the music from various FM stations. No calls came in on his car phone, which was fine with him. It meant everything was copacetic in the world and no one would be late for this morning's meeting. Any calls at his Justin Steel phone number at home would be routed to his portable phone for the duration of his absence. The closer he was to his destination, the more gray the sky became. The gathering clouds appeared ominous, like a cancer of the heart. By the time he pulled into the IHOP parking lot, the snow flurries began.

He got out of the car, locked it, looked around, then advanced to the restaurant entrance. Though he was fifteen minutes early for the nine AM meeting, he saw

Mike Collins signaling to him from a window booth. A young lady was with him.

Steel took off his topcoat, folded it, and laid it in the booth, as he slid in next to it, opposite Mike and the girl. Mike extended his hand across the table and the men shook hands.

"How're you doing, Steel?" asked Mike Collins.

"Good. And you?" said Steel.

"Justin Steel," said Mike. "meet Sabina Rockwald."

"Please call me Sibby, Mr. Steel," she said, polite, but not smiling.

"Just Steel," he said.

"I'm sorry. Mr. Collins told me to address you as just Steel, but I forgot. It won't happen again - Steel." She smiled.

Justin Steel put great stock in first impressions and he felt positive about the vibes he received from across the table, first, from Mike Collins, who he had known for a long time, and next, from Sibby Rockwald, who he just met.

Mike Collins was short and sat slouched over. He was thirty-five and a bit overweight. His brown hair was thick all over and curly along the sides. His bushy eyebrows made his face look even pudgier than he really was. He looked nothing like what one might expect of an Illinois Bureau of Investigation agent. He had a good heart, a lot of common sense, a keen mind, and his accumulated wisdom seemed to show in his brown eyes. He looked like a man you could trust.

In the file Steel had read concerning Sibby, the photograph didn't do her justice. At eighteen, she was no longer a girl, but a woman. She sat erect, and sitting, seemed taller than Mike Collins. She had blue eyes, long straight. blonde hair, and wore no make-up. Still, her lips were pink and full. Her complexion was fair and she looked as if she would burn easily if she stayed out in the sun too long. Her eyes were puffy as if she'd recently cried and she put her upper teeth over her lower lip as if not wanting to say the wrong thing. Her head was considerably smaller than Mike's and though her face appeared round, her body seemed slender. She was five foot, six, and though she didn't stand, Steel tried to imagine how she might look.

Since his wife, Genevieve, died twelve years ago, Steel sought no female companionship. But now, as he looked across the table, this young woman stirred something within him. She looked nothing like his petite wife from another lifetime.

He scolded himself for betraying, even momentarily, the memory of his wife. He still thought of himself as married. Perhaps, he thought, Sibby could be the daughter he never had. He felt more at ease with that thought.

"I have phone calls to make," said Mike Collins. "this'll give you two a chance to talk. I already ate. so you can order for yourselves. I'll be back in an hour." Steel appreciated Mike's giving him a chance to talk with his potential client alone.

Through the restaurant window, Steel watched Mike head toward his green Buick Regal that was now almost completely hidden by the heavier falling snow. Without cleaning off his car, Mike drove out of the parking lot and out of sight. As Steel returned his gaze toward Sibby, he noticed her growing agitation.

"Are you okay?" he asked.

"It's the snow," she said. "It snowed that night."

48

"Do you want to talk about it," he asked.

"Only if I have to," she said, fidgeting in her seat.

"I think I have most of the facts," he said. "Tell me only what you want to, whatever seems most important." He reached for her hand above the table, to reassure her, to relax her. She pulled it away. He leaned back, uncomfortable.

"That bastard killed my family," she said, with emphasis on the bastard.

"Who?" asked Steel. He knew who she meant but he thought it was important for her to say it.

"You know damn well who," she said in a loud voice, her face reddened.

Some heads in the restaurant turned toward them, then returned to their eating when there was nothing further to look at.

A waitress came to their booth. "Are you ready to order?" she droned.

"Coffee for now," said Steel. "More orange juice, Sibby?" he asked. She nodded her head. Her teeth bit into her lower lip. "Give us a few minutes to order," he said to the waitress. She walked away shaking her head, her pencil tucked into her hair above her ear.

"Tell me who you think killed your family," repeated Steel.

Sibby leaned her head forward, looked to her side, then back to face Steel. "Brad 'fucking' Kendall," she whispered. She sat back in her seat again.

Steel was taken aback by her intensity.

"How do you know it was him?"

"I saw him with my eyes." She pointed to her eyes. "I saw the bloody knife in his hand. I watched him run from me. I chased him but he got away."

49

"Did you see him kill your family members?"

She glared at Steel with squinted eyes. "No," she said.

"Did you see or hear anyone else?"

"No."

"Did Brad say anything to you?"

"Yes. He said he was sorry."

"Anything else?"

"No." She was trembling, but he didn't reach over to comfort her.

The waitress came with the coffee and juice and saw Sibby's angry face. She looked at Steel who sat silent. The waitress cleared her throat before she spoke.

"Would you like to order now or should I come back?" she said sarcastically.

"Bring the number two and the number four," said Steel, trying to be rid of her.

"How would you like your eggs?"

"Scrambled?" he looked at Sibby. She shrugged. "Scrambled," he repeated to the waitress.

The waitress seemed satisfied and walked away.

The respite with the ordering seemed to have calmed down Sibby. Steel had more questions, but he proceeded cautiously.

"Did you see your parents and brother and sister after they were killed?" He waited.

"Yes," she said. Steel flinched at her apparent pain.

"Was it after or before you saw Brad at the front door?"

"After."

"I'm sorry I have to ask you these questions," said Steel. "I know how hard it must be for you."

"How would you know how I feel. Everybody asks the same questions over and over and they all say they know how hard it is for me. They don't know and you don't know." She was in tears.

"I know," he said. He didn't generally discuss his family with people, especially clients, especially during the initial meeting. But this situation was different. A loss of an entire family, in an instant. They both had that in common. So he told her. And when he finished, he himself was near tears. She reached across the table and took his trembling hand in hers.

Their eggs, pancakes, potatoes, and toast were set before them. They removed their hands from the table. The waitress saw their teary eyes and remarked, "All better now?" And left the check.

"What do you want of me?" he asked.

"To hire you," she said.

"And what do you want me to do?"

"To find the killer of my family. To find Brad Kendall."

"And if he didn't do it?" asked Steel.

"He did it and I want him to pay," she said.

Unconsciously, they started to play with their food, taking bites here and there.

"What if I find someone else killed your family? What then?" asked Steel.

"It was him," she said.

"Why didn't he kill you? You were the only witness."

"... I don't know."

"I'll do my best to find who killed your family. I promise," said Steel.

"I can't pay you," she said.

"Don't worry about that," he said.

"That's what Mr. Collins said you would say." They both smiled. Steel became more convinced that he wouldn't rest until he found the killer.

In general terms, he explained that he would work only for her, that their conversation was between them. He said he would talk to her Uncle and Aunt, her friends, and keep her appraised of what she should know. He would check into her father's business endeavors and learn what he could. By the time Mike Collins returned, they were eating pleasantly and making casual conversation.

"How'd it go?" asked Mike.

"Fine," they said, with their mouths full of food, and laughed.

"I need to talk to Steel for a minute. Could you excuse us, Sibby?" he said. They walked toward the entryway of the restaurant out of her earshot, and out of the way of traffic.

"I have a lead for you," said Mike Collins. "But I'm afraid its cold."

"What is it?" asked Steel.

Mike reached into the breast pocket of his suit coat and retrieved a postcard mailed to Sibby at her parents' address. To protect it during handling, Mike had it enclosed in a plastic wrap. It read: "Sibby, I'm so sorry for your losses. It looks bad for me, I know. I have to keep moving. I love you." It was signed by Brad and was postmarked in Brodhead, Wisconsin.

"We intercepted this communication three weeks ago. We didn't show it to her," said Collins, as he pocketed the evidence.

They returned to the table. Steel gave Sibby his private telephone number for her use, alone. Mike was surprised because he knew how closely Steel guarded that number. Mike agreed to drive Sibby home, so Steel excused himself. On the way to his car, he trudged through two inches of snow that had fallen in the past hour. He started the Taurus, then stepped out to clean it off, while it warmed up. He got in again and drove into the slow moving traffic.

# Chapter 6

The snow viciously blew into his eyes and the wet blood on his clothes froze onto his skin as Brad Kendall frantically ran from the scene of the murders. He never witnessed death up close before, but tonight he saw four bodies and their blood clung to his clothes and hands. In his panicked flight from the Rockwald home, he had gone a block past where he parked his Ford. He doubled back, fumbled with the car keys, started it up, and skittered away.

Because of the snow storm, the streets were empty. With the wipers slapping back and forth, the windshield stayed clear, but Brad couldn't see past the hood of the car as the headlight beams reflected back off the falling snow. For two blocks, he drove aimlessly, then decided he should go to his house to clean up. The ride home took a long ten minutes as he stayed on side-streets and carefully drove the middle of the slick road.

His parents could be home from the movies soon so he had to hurry. He didn't want to meet up with them. He frenetically discarded his bloody apparel into a paper bag which he left in the bathroom. A minute for a shower was all he could spare and he noticed when he dried himself, he left imprints of unwashed blood on the towel.

He put on clean underwear, sweat socks, jeans, flannel shirt, and dry black Nike cross-trainers. Into a duffel bag he packed extra clothing and toiletries. He had two hundred dollars in his top dresser drawer and he pocketed the money. Donning his parka and snatching his duffel bag, he rushed out the front door. The phone began to ring but he didn't go back to answer it.

He leaped into his car and stepped on the gas peddle with such ferocity that it lurched into the street. His wheels were spinning, causing the car's back end to sway from side to side, until he got control of it again. He knew he had to get away but he didn't know where to go. He remembered the bloody clothes he left behind but it was too risky to go back for them.

He suddenly realized he could never go back. He couldn't think of where he could go that he wouldn't be found. Surely, Sibby would turn him in. They would surely get his license plate number. He reasoned the snow could be his ally by making his plates difficult to see. Even if he resorted to public transportation, he could just as easily be spotted. He decided to stay with the car.

Which way should he go? This was the question he asked himself. Which way would they expect him to go?

He had no answer. For no obvious reason, he headed north on Route 41. The snow was relentless but he decided this was good for him, as long as he didn't break down or get stuck. He tried the radio, figuring AM would have the news more often. Initially, the talk was only of the ominous weather. But, at ten-thirty, WMAQ reported multiple murders in a northern suburb and promised more news later. Flipping to the other stations brought no additional information.

His fuel gauge indicated he was almost out of gas. He would have to risk stopping. Somewhere after passing Lake Forest, he was able to pull into a station that was open twenty-four hours. He kept the car running while he filled the tank, went inside to pay the fifteen dollars, and with no exchange of words between himself and the young male attendant, returned to his vehicle and took to the road again. After he pulled out, he wished he had remembered to buy candy bars or snacks.

He had just driven past Gurnee and Six Flags Great America amusement park, when the eleven o'clock news blurted out the highlights of the murder of an entire family in affluent Glen-Deer, and that police, already spread thin because of the numerous highway accidents, were attempting to ascertain what had occurred. More details were promised as they became available.

Brad was exasperated at his inability to make better time because of the horrible driving conditions, but he also realized that the weather was excellent cover for him. Very few cars were on the road now. Whoever needed to get home had already done so and who had no urgency to be out, wisely stayed home.

His adrenaline rush had played itself out. He was tired of driving, was hungry, and needed to go to the bathroom. Yet, he knew he had to plod on; it was his only hope of escape.

If he had it to do over again, he wouldn't have gone to see the Rockwalds tonight. He couldn't help what had happened. Worse still was that Sibby had to see him leaving. *Poor Sibby,* he thought. *She deserved better. The Rockwalds deserved better.*

Brad thought of his parents, how hurt they would be. They would find the bloody bag of clothes. Then, they would hear about the Rockwalds. The police would probably question his folks and accuse them of hiding their son. In the end, they would be able to do nothing but feel guilty and ashamed.

And Brad Kendall could do nothing, except flee, and hope he wouldn't be caught. He had to keep moving while he could, under the cover of the storm. For soon, it would be morning, and it would be light, and there would be nowhere he could hide.

# Chapter 7

After he left the IHOP, Justin Steel drove north on Route 50 until it joined with Route 41, and headed in the same direction. The fierce snow, propelled by the powerful northeast wind, came off Lake Michigan and was wet and heavy despite the cold of January. The traction of his Taurus was exemplary as long as he exercised patience and caution in his journey to the Glen-Deer police station.

It was past eleven when he pulled into the municipal parking lot next to the building that housed the mayor's office, the water department, and the police station. Due to the suddenness of the heavy downfall, the lot had not yet been plowed and he wasn't sure if he parked in a restricted area.

He was clad in suit, tie, topcoat, and dress shoes. Behind the seat, he kept over-the-shoe galoshes, that he slipped on. He reached for the Bears' cap he had tucked in the glove compartment. To keep them dry, he placed his bifocals into the case he kept in his suit coat breast pocket. He had to trudge at least a hundred feet to the front door and he didn't want to be uncomfortably wet the rest of the day.

He gained entry through the glass double-doors and stepped into the foyer where he deposited his wet galoshes and cap. He shook the snow off his topcoat and hung it on a rack. He smoothed his hair, slipped his glasses back on, and approached the reception desk with the confidence and respectability this community of citizens of above average wealth emanated. The median-priced home in Glen-Deer commanded three times the price that a home in Chicago or Skokie did, but only half as much as one in Lake Forest or Kenilworth. Steel felt pretty much at home.

He had spotted the name on the wall plaque when he walked in so he asked for Chief McElroy by name.

"I'm sorry, sir," said the pudgy, middle-aged receptionist with the high-pitched voice and excessively made-up face. "Chief McElroy retired in November."

"I see," said Steel, undaunted. "Do you have a new chief?"

"No sir, not yet," she said. "But we do have an acting chief, Lt. Banks. Would you like to see him?"

"Yes," said Steel.

"May I tell him what this is in regards to?" she whined.

"It's a personal matter," said Steel.

"Sir," she said, rather surly. "I have to tell him something."

"Tell him it's about an ongoing case."

"Your name, sir."

"Justin Steel."

"Wait here, sir. I'll see if he's in."

Steel gave her his best smile.

Moments later, a tall man, about thirty-five, slender, but broad in the shoulders, in full uniform, approached, and extended his hand.

"Fred Banks, here. What can I do for you?"

"My name is Steel. I would like to speak with you about an ongoing case."

"Which case," asked Banks.

"Could we talk in your office?" Steel turned toward the receptionist who had been eavesdropping. She lifted up her nose and walked away.

"I only have a few minutes," said Banks, who led him to a small office containing a gray metal desk, and pointed to a gray metal folding chair for Steel to sit in.

"State your business," said Banks, as he seated himself behind the desk n another gray chair.

"I've been hired by Sabina Rockwald to look into the murder of her family. I realize this is an ongoing case and I want to fully cooperate with you. I'm proficient and professional at what I do."

"How and why did Ms. Rockwald come to you?" asked Banks.

"She was referred to me by state agent, Mike Collins."

"You know Mike?" perked up Banks.

"Yes," said Steel.

"You don't mind if I check with him, do you?" said Banks.

"Go right ahead," said Steel, knowing Banks didn't need his permission. "Try his car phone if you want to reach him now. Here's his number." Steel handed Mike's business card to Banks.

Acting Chief Banks turned the Rolodex on his desk and located Collins' name. He matched the information with the card Steel gave him. "We don't have his car phone marked. I'll write it in now. Would you wait here while I step out?" he said.

"No problem," Steel said.

Two minutes later, Fred Banks walked back into the room where Steel waited for him. "He spoke  highly of you and asked us to cooperate with you and since I can't think of any reason not to, we'll try to provide you with what we can."

"I appreciate it," said Steel.

"What do you want to know?" asked Banks.

"Do you have any suspects besides Brad Kendall?" asked Steel.

"How much do you know?"

"Only what Mike Collins and Sabina Rockwald told me." Steel didn't mention the file he received from the FBI.

"Kendall is our primary suspect. We have his prints on the murder weapon and at the scene. He and Sabina recently broke up and he made threats to Sabina and the dead father. Kendall looks good for it. Problem is, he's disappeared."

"Where have you looked for him?" asked Steel.

Fred Banks looked at Steel, paused, then spoke. "I'm new as acting chief. I caught the case because no one here knew what to do. To tell the truth, this is a small town. We're not up for it. We do traffic, B and E's, and domestics. We . . . I called for help. Soon, we had the Staties, the Feds, the press, and everybody's tripping over one another. We're pretty certain Kendall's not in town. Once he left our jurisdiction, we were totally reliant on outside help, but nobody seems to be able to find him."

"Mind if I look?" asked Steel.

"Knock yourself out," said Banks.

"Does anybody else look good for it?" asked Steel.

"Not like the kid," said the acting chief. "We questioned Frank Rockwald, the brother, Sabina's uncle, the one she's staying with, because he had motive. Sabina doesn't know, so tread carefully. It appears that the deceased Richard Rockwald and Frank's wife were having an affair."

Steel squinted.

"The brother had enough reason to do it but he was someplace else that night," said Banks.

"Anybody else?" said Steel.

"Nobody, really," said Banks. "We thought about Sabina's implication but we ruled her out. We also know Richard Rockwald owed some money, but nothing big, a few thousand, maybe. We found no evidence of breaking and entering or burglary. Nothing seemed to be missing. We, the Staties, and the Feds turned the place upside down. Poor Sabina couldn't even go home to that mess. Why would she want to? I wouldn't. It's better for her at her uncle's. I guess. At least for a while. I think the house is in foreclosure, anyway. Good luck selling it." Banks looked up. "What else do you need?"

"Do you have a key for the house and can I go see it today?" asked Steel.

"We've got several sets." Banks walked to a file cabinet and took a key out of a folder. "Take this one

63

and when you leave, lock it in the house. Put it on the kitchen sink. No sense coming back in this weather. I'll need your business card and if I can see your ID?"

Both satisfied, they shook hands and agreed to keep each other informed. Banks walked him to the entryway where Steel retrieved his boots, coat, and cap.

It had stopped snowing, but it was still overcast and cold. Steel rubbed his left arm that was stiffening with the weather. Best to keep moving, he thought to himself, as he headed to the murder scene.

# Chapter 8

It was two AM and Brad Kendall had been driving for over three hours. He was exhausted and he wanted to sleep but it was too cold to sleep in the car. He was now on Route 11 and he was proceeding west when he spotted a lonely, blinking sign which should have read *Eagle Lake Motel*, except the 'el' was not illuminated, so what he saw was *Eagle Lake Mot.* He pulled into the unplowed, snow-filled lot and parked as far from the office that he could. He grabbed his duffel bag and plodded through ten inches of accumulated snow and found the office unlocked.

There was a buzzer on the counter and a sign instructing any visitor to press it. Brad pushed the button and heard its reverberation in the next room. He waited patiently and a minute later an elderly man, about seventy, shuffled in with slippers on. The man's glasses sat at the tip of his beaked nose and he looked over them at who had woke him.

"What can I do for you?" he said in a course voice not yet fully awake. He brushed the few gray hairs on his head to one side as he approached the counter that separated himself and Brad.

"I'm sorry to wake you," said Brad. "But I need a room, please." His voice shivered as he said the words.

"That's okay, son. It's my job. Out a little late, aren't we?"

"Yes, sir. Slow driving out there. Bad weather, you know," said Brad.

"Where you headed?" said the gent, as he pushed his glasses in place.

"Ugh . . . Madison," said Brad, the only town in Wisconsin he could think of at the time.

"Go to school there, do you?" asked the elderly innkeeper, as he fiddled with some registration cards and searched for a pencil.

"Ugh . . . visiting a friend. He goes to school there."

"We'll fix you up with a room right soon here, son. Just fill out this card. Will this be credit card or cash?"

"Cash," said Brad.

Brad started to write his real name, then caught himself. Instead, he wrote Brent Kelly. He gave a Chicago address and wrote in a phony license plate number. That's why he parked as far from the office that he could, so his plate wouldn't be read easily. There was room for about twenty cars in the lot and his was only the third.

"Where'd you park your car, son?"

"Way at the other end, sir . . . so's I wouldn't get in the way of the guys who plow your lot. Okay?" said Brad.

"That's real considerate. People your age are usually so rowdy, so rude. It's a pleasure having you here with us," he turned the card to see the name on it. Mr. Kelly.

"That's thirty-two dollars for a single. It's a nice room. Got its own thermostat and a color TV that works."

"Can I pay now?" asked Brad. "In case I need to leave early, so I don't wake you, again."

"See what I mean, real thoughtful," said the man.

Brad took his receipt and a key for room twelve. He noticed some vending machines so he bought a Snickers Bar and a Dr. Pepper.

The room was halfway down the long, one-level, frame building. The snow was piled up to the front door since the overhang couldn't keep most of it away. He let himself in, hit the light switch, then double-bolted himself in.

Brad set his duffel bag in the corner of the room, put his candy bar and soft drink on the dresser, then went to the bathroom. After he popped the room thermostat to seventy degrees, he pulled the on-switch of the television set, but all the stations had gone off the air for the night.

He was hungry, but mostly he was tired, so he decided to leave the Snickers and the Dr. Pepper for morning. Stripping down to his shorts, he threw back the covers, jumped in, and waited for his bed and the room to warm up. He thought he would fall asleep immediately, but his body quivered from over-excitement, and his mind was in overdrive. Since he had no alarm clock to wake him, he worried about sleeping too late in the morning, and he didn't want to ask the office to wake him. It never occurred to him, that as exhausted as he was, he would have trouble falling asleep.

The lamp light beside his bed was still on and though he had forgotten to shut it off before he had gotten under the covers, he realized he was afraid to make it dark. His eyes remained open and refused to shut for sleep.

Once again, he saw the bodies of Richard and Donna Rockwald, perforated with stab wounds. as they laid, next to each other, in one another's blood. The knife was once more in his hand and he recoiled from the thought as he forced himself to look under his blanket, to see if it was there. He couldn't remember how the knife had gotten into his possession, or to whom it belonged. He didn't own it but he couldn't deny he held it.

The cries from Cindy and Richie Rockwald's bedrooms distracted him from his hellish reverie. He hurried to their rooms, the knife still in his hand, and all he could remember was that they were dead when he left their beds.

A noise at the front door startled him. A voice calling, one he recognized - Sibby. He rushed to the house doorway, the entrance to hell, to prevent her from seeing the devil's carnage. "I'm sorry, Sibby," he heard himself cry out. He visualized himself apologizing while still clutching the bloody knife. He watched the knife drop to the floor. He heard her scream to get away. Her accusation of him jolted his sensibility, so he ran from her ranting condemnation to the protective shelter of the white blizzard as she continued to rail after him.

Eventually, like snow, a white blanket of repose covered his eyes, and with the light still on, he fell into a fitful sleep. He was running down a snow-laden but deserted street and was being chased by Cindy and Richie with a monopoly game under his arm, a game they often played together.

A voice from the sky boomed at him, "Stay away from my daughter," the voice of Richard Rockwald.

The snow from the trees began to melt into the street as he ran, only it melted red, like blood, and turned the road crimson. Brad sloshed through the blood, no longer able to run, his feet in slow-motion. He screamed but no sound came from his mouth. A roar behind him, chasing him, getting closer, getting louder, and he fell under its weight.

Brad Kendall was on the motel room floor, tangled in his blankets, and he heard the snow plow clearing the parking lot outside his door. He walked to the window, moved the heavy curtain an inch, and saw that it was morning. It was so bright, that his sleep-stupored eyes squinted from the painful intrusion of light.

He looked at his watch and it was eight o'clock. His fear of oversleeping had been realized. There was no time to shower so he washed his face and brushed his teeth. He watched the TV while he dressed. He clicked channels until he found the news. Shocked, he saw his picture on the screen. He turned up the volume.

The female news commentator described a ghastly murder of a family of four and Brad Kendall was being sought for questioning. She gave his height as six-three, his weight as two fifty-five, his hair color as brown, his eyes as green and his complexion as ruddy. She also gave the car he was driving and its license plate number.

In panic, Brad switched to the other stations but all he got was talk shows and exercise programs.

Brad finished dressing, repacked his duffel bag, throwing in the candy bar and soda. Buttoning his parka, he donned his gloves and was ready to go. He knew he had to leave the car. He couldn't risk driving it or moving it. Hoping the old man who checked him in, was sleeping, or didn't watch TV, or didn't make the connection to him, Brad figured he had until noon to distance himself from the car. As long as the old man saw the car was still in the parking lot, he would assume Brad decided to sleep late. Since noon was check-out time, somebody would probably knock on the door about that time.

With about one hundred-fifty dollars in his wallet, Brad had no idea how far or where it would take him as he started on foot toward the highway, trying to leave unnoticed. He figured he had to get to a bus or a train station somewhere. As he walked beside the snow piled along the road, a passing semi-truck pulled next to him.

"Need a lift?" the driver hollered through the open passenger side window.

"Yeah, thanks," said Brad. "My car broke down and I had to leave it at a repair shop while they ordered parts," he lied.

"Where you headed?" asked the trucker.

"Madison," said Brad, sticking to his lying. Actually, he had no idea where he was going.

"I can take you as far as Janesville," barked the driver who said his name was Bill.

"I'm Bob," Brad continued to lie. "And Janesville is great."

"I got some coffee in a thermos. Want some?" said Bill.

"No, thanks," said Brad. "I've already had breakfast. I'll just have the candy bar and pop from my bag."

# Chapter 9

Justin Steel pulled up to the curb in front of the Tudor style house on Red Bud where the Rockwalds had been murdered. It was early afternoon, the clouds had begun to disburse, but the sun was so low in the winter sky, that its heat couldn't warm the earth. Tonight, without cloud cover, the temperature was scheduled to plummet. But now, the sun brought out the brightness in the snow and its glazed surface caused Steel to squint at the house.

Steel made virgin tracks in the snow as he made his way up the stairs to the front door. It opened easily when he turned the key. He removed his galoshes in the entry way but kept his coat on since it didn't seem much warmer inside the house. A chill trickled up his backside when he noticed the dried blood that still remained on the entryway door trim.

He entered the living room and saw the mess that had been left behind. Cushions lay askew along the sofa that sat at an unnatural angle from the wall. Framed pictures and paintings leaned against the wall along the floor, instead of hanging where they should. Muddy footprints covered the rug and gum wrappers and other fragments of paper were strewn about.

The kitchen and dining room were no better. Chairs lay on their sides. Cabinet doors and drawers were left open all the result of thoughtless law enforcement personnel, all of which could have been cleaned and straightened up, thought Steel.

What couldn't be made right was what happened in the bedrooms. He entered the first bedroom and saw Michael Jordan and Walter Payton posters on the wall. Boys clothing hung in the closet; Richie's room. The mattress had been removed from the room by the forensic people, but the bed frame remained.

The bedroom next to it was painted pink, with a pink dresser, and a pink bed to match. The mattress was missing in this room as well. A Ryne Sandberg poster hung on the wall. In the closet, a twelve-inch softball and fielders glove sat on a shelf above the jeans and tee shirts on plastic hangers. Not quite a woman; not finished being a child; never to reach her potential. Steel couldn't linger too long; memories tried to force themselves into his brain.

The third bedroom on this side of the house was relatively undisturbed. The bed was carefully made up on a mattress that obviously had not been taken. The closets and the dresser drawers were empty except for a few hangers that were on the floor. Nails in the wall remained where pictures had once hung. Steel surmised this had been Sibby's room and that she had taken her possessions to her uncle's house, or more likely, someone had done it for her.

Steel walked across the length of the house to the master bedroom. The king-size mattress was missing. Dresser drawers had been left open in varied positions. Clothing was scattered about. It looked like someone had attempted to wash away the blood from the wall above the bed, but it remained, and Steel surmised, would always remain, whether visible to the human eye or not.

He thought of his house, where his family had been killed. Perhaps it was better that the house had burned to the ground. No one should be forced to live where a murder had occurred. He knew he couldn't.

Steel walked around the rest of the house. He looked in closets, checked windows, tried doors, and felt fabrics and carpets. He didn't expect to find anything that the other trained investigators couldn't find. He just had to see for himself, get a feel of the crime and the passion of the moment. He had to consider avenues of entry and escape. What was possible; what was not. What could have happened and what was not likely.

He considered escape routes. There were three doors that led to the outside. Besides the front entry, there was a door in the kitchen that led to the back yard. A side door that accessed the office Richard Rockwald used was also a way in and out of the house. A dozen or more windows were reachable from the ground. All an intruder needed was a three-step ladder that could easily be carried. Most of the windows opened easily and half of these allowed simple maneuvering of the tracked storms and screens on the outside.

Like today, it snowed heavily the night of the killings. Anyone could easily have come into the house earlier and left without a trace since the fresh snow today, as on that night, would have covered any evidence of approach and exit.

Steel didn't bring a camera to record what he examined. What he needed to remember, he felt he could recall. He had seen what he had come to see and perhaps more than he wished he had. Whatever else may be true, it would probably be best for Sibby not to return to this house again.

# Chapter 10

It was a little after four when Steel checked into the Holiday Inn in Skokie. He carried in all his luggage and the box containing the information concerning the Rockwald investigation. He could work in his room, make necessary telephone calls, eat without leaving the building, and with the snow and the cold outside, this seemed a good idea. In the morning, the workout facilities the hotel provided would be beneficial to him as well.

The first call he made was to Gus and Emily Hessmuller. He informed them that he would be gone several days, at least, and would keep in touch with them as he was able. There was plenty of food available for them and Scrap Iron.

His other calls, to Frank Rockwald, Sibby's uncle, and to Brad Kendall's parents, would best be made in the evening, after they had come home from work. His stomach was telling him he had not eaten since morning, and that it was time for food.

The Holiday Inn dining facilities were not exquisite, but they were more than adequate. He ordered what he normally couldn't prepare at home. He remembered their excellent chicken pot pie, accompanied by a reasonably stocked salad and soup bar, so that is what he ordered.

Upon returning to his room, he watched the evening news on TV. Nothing significant had occurred today, the weather would remain cold and no more snow was expected. Because his arm had stopped aching, he agreed with the weatherman's prognosis. The Bulls would play later tonight. Nothing else was happening on this January night.

He telephoned Frank Rockwald who picked up on the fifth ring. After explaining who he was, Steel asked if they could meet for breakfast tomorrow. Rockwald already had a breakfast appointment but they agreed on lunch at Moby Dick's, a restaurant and bar, that specialized in seafood. It was located across from Frank Rockwald's insurance sales office and just minutes from the Holiday Inn.

Steel next dialed Brad Kendall's parents. Mrs. Kendall picked up on the first ring. When she said, "hello," Steel could sense urgency in her voice, as if she was expecting a call, or was taking a call she didn't want.

"Mrs. Kendall, my name is Justin Steel. Is Mr. Kendall able to come to the phone?"

"He's not home from work, yet," she said warily. "What is it you want?"

"I would like to meet with you and Mr. Kendall, as soon as possible."

"Why?" she asked.

"I would like to find your son, Brad, and I hoped you could help me."

"Are you with the police?" she asked.

"No, I'm not. I work privately, and I'm trying to help the police and perhaps help your son."

"Help my son - how? By putting him in jail?"

"That's not my job - to put anybody in jail, including your son. I just want to talk to him."

"I don't know where he is. We, my husband and I, don't know anything - except that a terrible mistake has been made. My son is a good boy. He wouldn't do anything wrong."

"I don't want to hurt your son. I just want to talk to him. Maybe we can work together to find who killed the Rockwalds and your son can be cleared. When can I meet with you and your husband?"

"In the evening," she said.

"How about tonight?" he said.

"No, not tonight," she said.

"How about tomorrow night, then?" he prodded. "How about seven?"

"All right," she said. "I suppose. We just want to clear our son."

Steel confirmed their address and was ready to hang up. But before he did, he could hear her crying.

He went down to the vending machine and returned with some snacks and soft drinks. He removed contents of the box of information he received from the FBI. He sorted the files into four stacks on the bed. One pile was for the grocery business the dead Richard

Rockwald owned; the second was for the bowling alley; the third was for the three pizza restaurants; and the fourth was for the import/export business.

Not all the income statements and balance sheets were current but what all the businesses showed was frequent draws on miscellaneous expense accounts and consequently, all were losing money. It was no wonder the businesses were in the red considering the vast amount of cash flowing out. An anomaly of the import/export business was the large amounts of sizable deposits that seemed to match the withdrawal amounts from the other enterprises.

All were set up as individually-owned, subchapter S, closely-held corporations, and as such, one corporation had nothing to do with the other, legally, except that the deceased Richard Rockwald controlled them all. All the businesses were technically bankrupt and could be declared as such by Richard Rockwald himself or by any of his creditors. Except, Rockwald was now dead, and they were doing the declaring.

Most of the money ended up in the import/export business, and was called simply, Rockwald, Import/Export, Inc. But where did the money that was withdrawn from this company go? Richard Rockwald was losing his house and his personal checking account was modest, so he didn't seem to have the money. Maybe he had it someplace else and was concealing it? But where? Steel, now wearing his Brisby accountant's hat, figured when he had that answer, other answers would fall in place. Like who killed the Rockwalds?

One other commonality occurred on all the balance sheets. A five thousand dollar liability on each of the four businesses, secured by a note, indicating Tertiary Affiliated as the creditor.

# Chapter 11

"Why did you agree to meet with him?" yelled Kenneth Kendall, Brad's father.

"He told me he might be able to clear Brad," said Brad's mother, Connie.

"Why would he want to clear our son when we know he works with the police and we don't even know why he's involved?" he said.

"I'm just telling you what he told me," she cried.

"He wants to trick us into telling him where Brad is," he said.

"How can we tell him" she said. "When we don't know where he is, considering he's been gone a month, and we haven't spoken with him in three weeks ?"

"That's the point," he said. "We know he was in Brodhead, Wisconsin, when he called us."

"He sounded so scared," she said. "I think he wanted to come home then."

"You know he couldn't," he said. "Everybody had him convicted already."

"But how can he clear himself, if he doesn't come home?" she sobbed.

"What if he really did it?" he said, catching himself as he spoke his thoughts aloud.

"How can you say that? How can you think that? This is our son. He's a good boy. I can't believe you feel he's guilty."

Immediately, he regretted revealing his inner thoughts. "I'm sorry, Connie. You're right. He couldn't have done it." He tried to console his wife, but she pushed him away and continued to cry.

"Maybe we should meet with this man - what's his name?" he asked.

"Justin Steel," she said.

"Let's meet with Mr. Steel and see if he really wants to help Brad," he said. "Or if he's like the rest who are trying to railroad our son."

# Chapter 12

Justin Steel woke up to the sound of the radio-alarm beside his bed. He shook off the sleep and the nightmare he'd been having. He put on his more presentable sweat clothes and headed three floors down to the Holiday Inn exercise room on the main level.

Half-an-hour later, he returned to his room and showered. Last night, he'd ordered breakfast to be brought to his room at six AM. When it arrived, he drank his orange juice and gazed out the window overlooking the parking lot. It was still dark out, but with the lot lights on, he could see that plows had cleared the snow around the parked cars.

He removed the lid from the eggs, bacon, and toast, and was glad his meal was still warm. As he drank his coffee, he checked his appointment calendar. At noon, he would meet with Frank Rockwald. Later tonight, he would be at the Kendall residence.

The problem with being up so early is that much of the rest of the world was sleeping, or on the way to work. It was nearly six-thirty, so he dialed Mike Collins on his car phone.

"Collins," was the answer after two rings.

"Steel, here. I thought you'd be sleeping," he said.

"So why'd you call?"

"Hopeful you would answer."

"No, *why* did you call? What can I do for you?" said Collins.

"Bad mood, today?" asked Steel.

"If you were sitting in this traffic jam, in unplowed snow, in the dark, you wouldn't be happy either," said Collins.

"Sorry, pal," said Steel. "I need a favor. Tertiary Affiliated. Richard Rockwald's businesses owed money to them. I'd like to know who they are."

"Spell the name for me," said Collins. Steel did.

Mike Collins promised to call him back in an hour. He said he would make a few phone calls from his car phone and by the time he got to his office downtown, the information would be on his desk.

When Steel gave Collins the telephone and room number he could be reached at, Collins joked, "Nice life."

"I deserve it," Steel joked back.

While he waited for the call from Mike Collins, he searched through the yellow pages for Dr. Anita Hart, the psychiatrist who was counseling Sabina Rockwald. He dialed the number and was greeted by a live answering service. Steel left his name, the number of the Holiday Inn, and used Sibby's name as a reference.

With nothing more he could do for the moment, he turned on the TV and watched the news on several stations, clicking channels back and forth. He had another cup of coffee and watched the sun come up over the frigid January horizon.

Forty-five minutes after he called her service, Dr. Anita Hart called Justin Steel back. "Who are you and what do you have to do with Sabina?" she asked.

"I'm looking after her interests but in a different way than you are, Doctor."

"That's an evasive answer," she snapped.

"I'm sorry," said Steel. "I didn't intend it to be. I understand how you are trying to help Sibby. I've had trauma in my life that required professional help like yours. I've been asked to help Sibby by finding the person or persons responsible for the deaths of her family members. In fact, I've been hired by Sibby. I just wanted you to know that."

"I thought Brad Kendall killed her family," said Dr. Hart.

"It's possible," said Steel. "But in my line of work, there are many variables."

"Mine, too," she said. "So, what are you? A lawyer? A detective?"

"I'm a private investigator."

"Why didn't you say that right-off?" she said.

"Good point," he said. "Is there anything you can tell me that would help me in my search for the killer?"

"Find Brad Kendall," she said.

"Anything else?" he asked.

"No," she said.

"Thanks for your help," he said, even though she had been no help at all. "I wanted you to know I also am trying to help Sibby."

"I'll take care of Sibby," she said, firmly.

"By the way," he said. "Who is paying for your services?"

"None of your business," she said.

"Actually, it is my business. I can find out. This isn't privileged information, so why don't you just tell me?"

"Her uncle, Frank Rockwald," she said after a pause. "Now if you have nothing further, I'm very busy."

"Thank you, Doctor. You've been a big help." After she hung up, he reasoned that she was only trying to protect her patient and he respected her for that.

A second after he hung up the phone, it rang again. It was Mike Collins.

"Got a pencil?" he asked.

"Shoot," said Steel.

"Tertiary Affiliated is licensed as a lender to businesses. Oddly enough, it's not set up as a corporation. It's a sole proprietorship under a DBA. The county shows the owner as Angelo Donofrio."

After Steel wrote down the downtown address and telephone number, he asked if Tertiary was a front. Mike Collins confessed that this was all the knowledge he possessed, but maybe the Feds knew more. Steel thanked him and they both hung-up.

Steel dialed the number Mike gave him, but a machine picked-up. It was probably too early to call and he didn't want to leave a message.

At eleven-thirty, he tried Tertiary again and this time a man answered.

"Tertiary Affiliated," he muttered.

"Angelo Donofrio," said Steel.

"Who wants him?"

"Steel."

"Say again."

"Justin Steel would like to talk to him."

"About what?" the man asked.

Steel paused for a few seconds, then answered, "About Richard Rockwald."

"Hold on," said the man.

A half-a-minute later, another voice said, "This is Angelo Donofrio. What can I do for you, Mr. Steel?" Whereas the first voice sounded gruff and terse, Donofrio spoke articulately and slowly.

"It's just Steel. No mister. I'd like to meet with you about Richard Rockwald and the money he owes you."

"Steel, you say - my, my." He was mocking him. "Are you calling to settle Mr. Rockwald's debts?"

"Could be?" said Steel.

"My office, tomorrow," said Angelo Donofrio. "Nine AM. Do you know where we are?"

"Yeah," said Steel.

# Chapter 13

Justin Steel arrived at Moby Dick's Restaurant and Bar at noon to meet Frank Rockwald as planned. Frank came from the bar and carried a Stinger to the table he and Steel were led to by the hostess.

"Sure you don't want a drink?" asked Frank.

"I'm sure," said Steel.

The dining area was poorly illuminated. Each table was adorned with candles providing just enough light to see the menu and tableware. An assortment of individually lighted paintings hung on the walls. Replicas of ships, the sea, and harpooned whales provided the motif. Authentic looking crossed harpoons and ragged fish nets further complemented the decor.

By the time they were seated, Frank Rockwald had finished his drink and signaled for another. Steel ordered coffee.

"We don't drink, do we?" said Frank.

"No, we don't," said Steel, knowing Frank was referring to him specifically. Frank did drink.

"Are we on the wagon?" Frank continued speaking in the plural.

"No," said Steel. "I'm working."

The comment brought sudden sobriety to Rockwald's demeanor. His hand trembled as he reached for his drink and sloshed it to his mouth.

"Sorry," said Frank. "Sometimes I ramble on without thinking." He set down his drink, wiped his mouth with a napkin, and looked Steel straight on.

"Why are we meeting," asked Frank.

"You know I represent Sibby. I told you that on the phone. I want to help her find who killed her family."

"I thought that was the job of the police," said Frank.

"I help," said Steel.

"Who pays you Mr. Steel?"

"Just Steel, " said Justin Steel. "I'm under contract to Sibby," he added.

"She has no money," said Frank.

"I know," said Steel.

"I'm not paying," whined Frank.

"I didn't ask you to."

Frank Rockwald fidgeted in his seat, nervously reached for his Stinger, then catching himself, withdrew his hand and placed it on his lap.

"Why do you care who killed my brother and his family?"

"Let's just say I care and leave it at that," said Steel.

"My brother is dead - Steel. You can't bring him back. Let it lie."

"I can't and I won't. Somebody has to pay; somebody has to be brought to justice," said Steel.

Frank Rockwald's face contorted with displeasure over the remark. "Who cares who did it? Finding the killer won't bring Richard back."

Steel decided to try a different approach to his interview.

"Did you know your brother was sleeping with your wife?"

Frank Rockwald hastily reached for his drink and in the process tipped it off the table. Glass shattered and liquid splattered on the carpet. Frank sheepishly drew back his clumsy hand.

A waitress hurried over to clean up the mess. She tried to assure Frank that it was all right and would he like a refill. Without speaking, he nodded his head.

Once the confusion ended, Frank glared at Justin Steel. "Who told you?"

"It's common knowledge," said Steel.

"Great. Just great," moaned Frank.

When the waitress brought the drink, he took it from her hand, and immediately downed half of it.

"Did it bother you that your wife was sleeping with your brother?"

"What the fuck do you think?" said Frank. "What a stupid fucking question." He bolted down the rest of his drink and held his glass above his head for the waitress to see.

She promptly brought a fresh drink and they traded glasses. She seemed quite willing to tolerate his abusive attitude as if he were a regular customer or a good tipper. Whatever her reason, she acted content to appease him.

"Did you confront your wife?"

"Yeah."

"What did she say?"

"That she was sorry."

"Did you forgive her?"

"Yeah."

"What about your brother?"

"What about him?"

"What did he say?"

Frank Rockwald lifted up his head and spoke as if bewildered. "He laughed at me."

"How did you feel about that?"

He looked at Steel, incredulously. "Like shit," he said. "Like I wanted to kill him," he offered.

"Did you kill him?"

"No, but I wish I had."

"So you're not sorry he's dead?"

"No," said Frank.

"How about Sibby?" said Steel. "How do you think this affects her?"

"I'm sorry for her." Frank's remark sounded sincere.

"Did she know about her father and your wife?"

"I don't think so. I hope not."

"Did the police question you about killing your brother?"

"Not really. They just asked me to account for my time."

"Did you," asked Steel.

"Yeah. I was with an insurance client."

"Were the police satisfied?"

"I guess so," mulled Frank.

"If you didn't kill your brother, who do you think did?"

"Sibby's boyfriend, I guess. I can't remember his name."

"Brad Kendall?" offered Steel.

"Yeah, him," said Frank.

"You're taking care of Sibby now, aren't you?"

"She's staying with me. Poor kid."

"Do she and you talk?" asked Steel.

"About what?" asked Frank.

"About anything."

"Mostly she talks with my wife. I got Sibby a shrink. Sibby seems okay, under the circumstances. But no, we don't talk much."

"How do you feel about Sibby hiring me?"

"She's a big girl. If that's what she wants."

"Is there anything else you can tell me?" asked Steel.

"Not really."

Frank ordered another drink, then started to cry. Steel decided to leave. He considered patting Frank's shoulder as a sympathetic gesture but thought better of it. As he looked back, he saw Frank with his head buried in his arms on the table.

# Chapter 14

Ken and Connie Kendall sat across from each other in their living room but didn't converse as they waited for their seven o'clock visitor to arrive. A minute after the hour, they heard the doorbell, and like two prize fighters, they leaped to their feet.

"I'll get the door," he said. She nodded and sat back down.

"Come in Mr. Steel," said Ken Kendall. "We're ready for you."

Steel followed the stoop-shouldered man to the living room. A silver coffee server had been set on a silver tray on the coffee table that separated the two green sofas that faced each other.

Ken sat down next to his wife on one of the sofas and motioned for Steel to sit across from them. Without asking, Connie poured into three clear glass cups set on clear glass saucers and handed one cup and saucer to

Steel. She pointed to the cream and sugar between them.

Connie Kendall's red-rimmed eyes showed signs of recent crying. She spoke first with a voice that quivered. "Tell us what you want, Mr. Steel."

Steel cleared his throat. "To find your son," he said with a gravelly voice. He took a sip of his coffee and set down the cup in front of him.

"Why?" she asked, her voice steady.

"To find out what he knows about the deaths of the Rockwalds."

"What you really mean is that you think he killed them," she said.

"I didn't say that."

"But you meant it."

Steel tented his fingers thoughtfully under his chin. "If your son is innocent, I want to help prove it."

"Ken and I want that, too, Mr. Steel," she said.

Steel went on. "And if he is guilty, I want to help him face up to what he has done."

The Kendalls became quiet. Connie began to cry. Her husband held her close to him and she didn't object.

Ken spoke. "Mr. Steel, we love our son and we believe he's innocent. We have to believe in his innocence. We won't condone what you're doing unless you believe in his innocence. Do you believe he's innocent, Mr. Steel?"

"I don't know," said Steel.

"Do you believe he's guilty?" asked Ken.

"I don't know that, either."

Connie sat up, dabbed at her eyes with a tissue, took a sip from her cup, then spoke. "So you have an open mind?"

"Yes," said Steel.

"But you work for Sibby Rockwald, don't you?" she said.

"Yes."

"What does she believe?" Connie asked.

"She thinks he killed her family."

Stunned, Connie slumped back in her seat. She sat upright again. "Did she witness the killings?"

"No," said Steel.

"Thank God," she said.

"So she doesn't know anything for sure, does she?" said Ken.

"And neither do I, Mr. Kendall. I may hurt your son or I may be able to help him."

"Call me Ken."

"Call me Steel."

"How can you help him?" asked Connie.

"If you believe your son didn't commit this crime, and that's what you're telling me, you'll want to help me find him."

"We believe in our son - Steel. He couldn't have done what they think he did. What you suspect he may have done," said Connie.

"Tell me where he is," said Steel.

Ken and Connie looked at each other, but neither spoke.

"Maybe he saw somebody. Or was a witness to the murders," said Steel.

The Kendall's faces perked up.

They looked at each other again. "We don't know," said Ken.

"Have you spoken with him? Did he call? Has he written?"

99

Connie spoke. "We talked on the phone about three weeks ago." Ken glared at her.

"He may be able to help Brad," she said. "We can't."

Ken stood up, put his hands to his head, and walked to the window. He looked out at the darkness.

"Brad called us from Brodhead - Wisconsin - told us not to worry - that he was all right," said Connie. "He sounded so frightened. He said he had to leave Brodhead, that he had to keep moving." She stared at nothing, and rambled on as if spilling out a confession. "His bus was leaving and he had to board. That's the last time we heard from him." She resumed her crying.

Steel didn't tell her he already knew about Brodhead. He let her continue to cry while Ken stared out the window. To Steel, Ken and Connie seemed like good parents, like good people.

Ken walked over to Steel. Ken had his hands tucked in his back trouser pockets. He took them out now and clasped them in front of him.

"Find our son, Steel. Bring him home to us. Please don't hurt him. Tell him we miss him and we love him."

"Yes," said Connie. "tell him we love him." She unexpectedly put her arms around Steel as if to vicariously hug her son, as if Steel could deliver her personal message.

Steel did all he could to keep from crying himself. He vowed to himself that if at all possible, he wouldn't hurt Ken and Connie and would try to bring their son back to them.

Steel left the Kendall household conflicted.

# Chapter 15

Justin Steel followed the tail end of the morning rush hour to downtown Chicago. He easily found the building he was looking for. It was just south of the Loop and the neighborhood appeared seedy, rough, and rundown.

The elevator didn't work so he climbed the stairs to the third floor. His appointment with Tertiary Affiliated was for nine and as usual, Steel showed up on time, a habit he acquired long ago.

The receptionist at the front desk was an overweight thug. He had his feet on the desk and his hands were clasped behind his head. He looked at Steel without changing position.

"Yeah, whataya want?" he said.

"I have a nine o'clock appointment with Mr. Donofrio," said Steel.

"Yeah? Says you."

Steel stepped close to the unkempt secretary and looked him in the eye. "Just tell him I'm here, pal."

He reluctantly put his feet down and stood up. He pointed to a chair and said, "Wait." He left the room while Steel remained standing.

A minute later, he returned and motioned for Steel to follow him. They walked single-file down a narrow hallway past three doorways until they reached a door at the end of the hall. The sign read, PRIVATE - DO NOT ENTER. They entered.

The room was poorly lit, but seemed to be decorated in good taste. There was a large mahogany desk with a red leather upholstered chair behind it. The walls were paneled in mahogany. The carpet was a deep red. Recessed lighting where the walls met the ceiling barely illuminated the somber room.

In a dark corner of the room sat a man with slightly gray hair and dark glasses. His legs were crossed at the knees and his hands were clasped on his lap.

"Did you bring the money, Mr. Steel?" inquired Angelo Donofrio.

"Just Steel."

"Yes, I forgot," he said. "You are a very bad man." He said this in a monotone and didn't change position or expression.

"I'm not bad. I just prefer Steel - Mr. Donofrio."

"Yes, that's right. You may call me Mr. Donofrio. Did you bring the money?"

"No," said Steel. "I would just like to know about Mr. Rockwald's indebtedness to you."

"Why?"

"To determine what his estate owes to you."

"There is no estate - Steel. Who are you? What do you want?"

"I'm someone looking into the death and debt of Richard Rockwald."

"That's very clever, Steel. You like to play with words. Now, get to the point. I'm busy."

"Rockwald owed you $5,000 from each of his four businesses."

"Ha," laughed Donofrio.

"What's funny?" asked Steel.

"It's considerably more, Steel."

"How much more?"

"If you don't know, it's none of your business."

"Were the loans secured?" asked Steel.

"Yes, Steel. With the life and honor of Richard Rockwald."

"So you killed him when he didn't pay?"

Donofrio paused and considered his response. "That's rather clumsy, Steel. A very poor choice of words. I'm offended."

"So what you're saying," said Steel, "is that you had someone kill him and his family for you."

"We're done," said Donofrio.

"Willie, show Mr. Steel out."

Willie grabbed Steel by the arm. Steel shook him away. "I have more questions, Mr. Donofrio."

Donofrio seemed unfazed and sat motionless.

From behind, Willie wrapped his arm around Steel's neck and tried to pull him to the door. "Let's go fucker," he said.

Steel twisted Willie's thumb on the hand he had wrapped around the neck. His stranglehold relaxed and Steel ducked under while continuing to twist the thumb until Willie went to his knees. Steel proceeded to knee Willie in the face.

Undaunted, muttering some unintelligible sounds, Willie got up and came for Steel. With sudden swiftness, Steel pushed the palm of his right hand into Willie's nose and bent it up into his eyes. Blood squirted on the red carpet.

Willie smeared the blood across his face and wiped it on his shirt and trudged toward Steel. "Fucker," he said. Only it sounded more like, "Pfugger." What Willie lacked in brains he didn't lack in courage.

Steel tired of Willie. With one quick swipe of the back of his open right hand, he caught Willie in the throat. Willie went down coughing, spitting blood, and gasping for air.

As if by reflex, Willie reached for his shoulder holster. Steel easily took the gun away from him and hit him across the back of his head with it. Willie slumped to the floor and stayed there.

Steel turned to face Donofrio and saw he had a revolver aimed at him. Steel held Willie's gun in his own hand.

"Calm down, Steel," he said. "Let's talk. I'll put down my piece if you do the same."

Steel had no desire to be shot or to shoot anyone. Warily, both men set their guns on the floor. Donofrio resumed his original position in his chair and Steel straightened his tie and tucked in his shirt.

"Willie's not my regular secretary, Steel. Clyde has the day off. I would like to have seen you work things out with Clyde. I wonder how that would've turned out."

"Let's hope we never find out," said Steel.

"Pity," said Donofrio.

"So tell me something about Rockwald's death," said Steel.

"I suppose you deserve an answer, Steel. You worked so hard for it." Donofrio looked down at the lump that was Willie.

"Rockwald owed us a lot of money and didn't try to pay it back. That wasn't very good business on his part."

"How much?" asked Steel.

"Not that it matters anymore, but in excess of two million dollars."

"What'd he do with that kind of money?" asked Steel.

"I'm sure I don't know, Steel. Spent it? Hid it? Who knows?"

"So you had him killed," said Steel.

"Not true, Steel. We had him scheduled for an early departure, but our representative discovered him already departed."

"So you say you didn't kill him?"

"How crude, Steel - that's correct. He was already gone."

"And the rest of his family?" asked Steel.

"They accompanied him."

"If you didn't do it, then who did?" asked Steel.

"We have quite a mystery, don't we?" Donofrio chuckled.

"I may be back," said Steel.

"The pleasure will be all mine," said Donofrio. "I hope you don't mind showing yourself out. Be careful. Don't trip on the trash."

When Steel exited, he left the door open.

Donofrio followed and locked the door from the inside. When he walked past Willie, he kicked him. "Get up, you useless shit." Willie didn't respond.

At his desk, Donofrio dialed out, then spoke. "We have a problem."

# Chapter 16

From his room at the Holiday Inn, Justin Steel called Mike Collins at the Illinois Bureau to inform him he was going to Brodhead in the morning. Steel brought him up to date on what had transpired over the past few days leaving out what he didn't want Mike to know.

"There's something else I should tell you," said Mike.

"Go ahead," said Steel.

"We recovered the car Brad Kendall was driving,"

"When was that?" asked Steel.

"Almost four weeks ago."

"Where'd you find it?" asked Steel.

"In Eagle Lake, Wisconsin. Kendall stayed at the Eagle Lake Motel for one night, the night of the killings. The owner of the motel called the local police the next day when he discovered the car abandoned and after he'd heard the news reports. The locals notified us a day or so later."

"So you had this information when you called me in, didn't you?" said Steel.

"I suppose," said Mike.

"You suppose?" Steel repeated in a stern voice.

"Okay, I knew," said Mike.

"When were you going to tell me?" asked Steel.

"We weren't supposed to release the information to anybody."

"So, I'm just anybody?"

"I didn't mean it that way," said Mike.

"How did you mean it?"

"All right. I could have told you - I should have told you," said Mike.

"You're damned right you should have told me," barked Steel.

"Sorry, Steel."

"What else haven't you told me?"

"That's it."

"You sure?"

"Yes," said Mike.

"Where is the car now and what did you find when you went over it?" asked Steel.

"It's impounded in Illinois. Forensics has gone over it carefully. They found traces of Richard and Donna Rockwald's blood and a third type. It doesn't match either of the Rockwald children but then again, they didn't bleed. It's assumed the blood belongs to Brad Kendall."

"Who talked to the motel owner?" asked Steel.

"The locals," said Mike.

"Do you have a copy of their report?"

"No," said Mike.

"No?" said Steel. "Why not?"

"We have a verbal report."

"You ever hear of fax machines?"

After a brief pause, Mike spoke. "Ease up a little, Steel. What the Feds have and what I have may vary. Local politics gets into the picture, too. That's why I suggested you be called in, to fill the gaps, to get the whole truth. That's the best I can tell you."

Steel considered Mike's explanation. Mike's sour voice told him that he had pushed him too far. "Okay. I'll do what I can," said Steel.

After Steel obtained the motel owner's name and the location of the inn, he and Mike ended their phone conversation amicably.

Steel dialed home and informed the Hessmullers that he would be on the road for a few days and would check back with them as he was able. They said the mail was piling up. He told them to keep stacking it.

He thought he should call Sibby and let her know what was happening but he wasn't decided on what she should know. As he debated in his mind, his private cell phone rang. It was Sibby.

# Chapter 17

Sibby Rockwald was near hysteria as she cried and shouted over the phone. Her utterances were incoherent. She ranted in incomplete sentences and thoughts. Finally, Steel was able to interrupt her ramblings.

"Calm down, Slow down. What is it?" said Steel.

"He called. He said I should make you stop investigating."

"Who called?" Steel asked.

"He said people die when they don't have to," she continued, still raving.

"Who called?" Steel repeated.

"He did. The man. I don't know who. A man."

"Stop," said Steel, sternly. "Take a breath. Start over again."

"A man called," she said. She'd stopped her sobbing.

"Who was he?"

"I don't know," she said.

"He threatened you?" asked Steel.

"Yes," she said. "I guess. I don't know. I suppose so. It sounded like a threat."

"Did he say anything else beside what you already told me?"

"No, that was all of it. Except, he repeated it several times, until I hung up on him."

"Did he call back?"

"No."

"When did he call?"

"A few minutes ago," she said.

"He didn't identify himself?"

"No," she said.

"What did he sound like?"

"Like a man. I don't know." He was losing her again.

"Think, Sibby. Did he sound young or old?"

"Old, I guess. I don't know."

"How did he talk? Fast or slow?"

"I'm not sure. Sort of jumbled."

"Jumbled?" said Steel. "I don't understand."

"Jumbled - like his words were mixed-up - like an accent," she said.

"Could you tell what kind of accent?"

"I'm not sure. I was so scared I was only hearing the words." Sibby's voice slowed, as if talking made her calmer.

"Did it sound like a European accent, like German or Polish or Italian?" Steel asked. "Or was it more like Canadian or Hispanic?"

"Mexican, I think," she said. "Yes, that was it. I'm sure of it."

"Good, Sibby," said Steel.

"Was he calling for himself or someone else?"

"I don't know," she said.

"And you don't remember anything else?"

"No, that was it. Maybe, I shouldn't have hung up?"

"That's okay. You did the right thing," said Steel.

"What should I do?" she pleaded.

Steel thought a bit, then suggested she carefully put down the phone and without showing herself, peek out the front window and see if a police car was sitting there. She said she was on a portable phone which she took with her to the window.

"Yes, there's a police car," she said.

"Good," said Steel, relieved. "Don't go out. Lock the windows and doors. I'll alert the police."

He waited as she did.

When she returned, he said, "Do you think it was Brad or one of his friends?"

"I'd know Brad's voice," she said. "And as far as I know, he has no Mexican friends."

"I just wanted to be sure," said Steel. "Is your uncle there?"

"No," she said.

"How about your aunt? Is she there?"

"Yes," said Sibby.

"Let me talk to her."

There was a hesitation on Sibby's part. "I don't think she can come to the phone. She's crying - hard."

"About your call?"

"No, something else. She and my uncle had an argument. He came home drunk. I'd never seen him this drunk. They fought for about an hour. I couldn't help overhear about her and my dad. I don't think I can stay

113

here anymore, Mr. Steel. Where can I go? I can't go home." Sibby was crying again.

"Oh, God," he said. *You poor kid*, he thought. She was right. She couldn't stay there, but she couldn't go home either. The only place he could think of was his home. With the Hessmullers, she might be comfortable and she definitely would be safer.

"I have some good people taking care of my home, Gus and Emily Hessmuller," he said. "You can stay with them."

"Would it be okay - I mean with my uncle - and you?"

"I'll talk to your uncle and I'm glad to do it. Are you okay with the arrangement?"

"I think so," she said. "I'm sure of it," she added.

"Listen carefully," he said. "Pack up your personal belongings, just what you actually need. Don't tell anyone where you're going. No one. In a few minutes, a police escort will pick you up. Ask for identification before you let anyone in. Understand?"

"Yes," she said.

After they hung up, Steel called Mike Collins and the Hessmullers again. Everything was arranged.

# Chapter 18

Justin Steel started out early in the morning when it was still dark and it didn't look like it was going to become daylight. He headed north on Route 41 toward Eagle Lake. The thought crossed his mind that it must have been the way Brad Kendall went that fateful December night.

It was nearly nine when Steel arrived at the Eagle Lake Motel. Beyond the motel itself, he could see a partially thawed body of water, probably the lake the town and the motel were named after. The parking lot he pulled into contained five cars. In back of the building, it was all woods and brush. The melting snow piles that surrounded the parking lot were dirty. The building looked to be in decent repair even though it had a lot of years on it. The word that came to Steel's mind was quaint.

He parked right in front of the office door. Out of the corner of his eye he could see a maid's cart sitting in front of one of the rooms near the far end of the building. From the door of the room it was less than five feet to a designated parking spot.

As soon as he walked through the door of the office, he smelled cooked bacon and freshly brewed coffee. The combined aromas reminded him that he hadn't eaten and was famished.

He pressed the button on the counter and it sounded in the adjoining room. A bent-over graying man walked through the parted curtains that separated one room from the other. He was chewing his food and adjusting his glasses as he stepped up to the counter and faced Steel. He motioned with his finger to wait and had one last swallow.

"Need a room, do ya?" he asked.

"I'm sorry I disturbed your breakfast," said Steel.

"Just finished," he said as he picked at some bacon between his teeth.

"How many of their are ya?" he asked.

"Just me," said Steel. "But I don't need a room. Just some of your time and some information."

The old man put down his pencil and looked over the top of his glasses at Steel. "What kinda information?"

Steel produced a business card and showed some identification. The old man looked at it then at Steel but didn't say anything.

"You had a young man, Brad Kendall, stay here about a month ago. He's the one who left his car in the lot, the one . . . ."

"I know who you're talkin' about," he said. I already talked to the police about him."

"I'm not with the police," said Steel.

"I can see that. What's your interest?"

"I work for the daughter of the people who were killed. I have to find Brad Kendall so I can talk to him."

"I'll tell ya right now," said the old man. "No way did the boy do what everybody's sayin' he did. No sir."

"What makes you say that?" asked Steel.

"The way he was, real polite, a real gentleman, ya know what I mean?"

"So you fancy yourself a good judge of character?" said Steel, making conversation.

"It's gotten me through life so far and I'm eighty-three years old and not too many people has fooled me yet."

"But some have fooled you? Is that what you're saying?" said Steel.

"This boy didn't seem like no rowdy to me. Paid cash, too. No credit card. Ya know what I mean?"

Steel wasn't sure what paying cash had to do with anything but to the old man it made sense. If anything, Brad Kendall wouldn't have used a credit card so as to avoid detection. Even writing a check might have revealed his location.

"Did Kendall register under his own name?" asked Steel.

"It's a funny thing. He used a fake name. Let me see here - I wrote it down - here it is - Brent Kelly. That's sure not right, usin' another name, is it?" said the old man.

"No, I think not," said Steel. "Did he say where he was headed?"

"He said, Madison. But maybe that wasn't true either, was it?" said the old man.

"Maybe. Maybe not," said Steel. "Do you think he talked to anybody else that was staying here that night?"

"We had only two other guests that night - bad snowstorm that night - bad for business, ya know. They were sleepin' when the boy got here. He got here real late. The police asked them some questions but they didn't know anythin', they said."

"Who called the police?" asked Steel.

"I did," he said.

"Why?"

"I told him, the boy, that checkout was noon. It was almost two so I knocked on his door but there was no answer. I figured he overslept, 'cause his car was still parked out front, ya know. But when I walked in, his room was empty."

"Did you call the police right away?" asked Steel.

"No reason to. He paid for his room. Figured he was someplace in town, just left his car here. No crime in that," he said.

"When did you call the police?"

"Next mornin'. My wife was watchin' TV - I never watch - she waved me over to come see about the murders. That's when I saw his picture. That's when I called the police. They come right over and took the car, ya know."

"Did Kendall talk to your wife or any of your employees?"

"He didn't talk to my wife and I got no employees. Just her. She's only sixty years old, ya know. A fine woman. Ya might of seen her in one of the rooms when

118

ya pulled up. My first wife ran off, but this one's a honey."

"Can I talk to her?" asked Steel.

"Won't do ya no good. She's deaf and dumb, and I already told ya, she didn't meet the boy."

"Is there anything else you can think of?" asked Steel.

"Nope. I told ya all I know."

"Are there any busses that go to Brodhead?"

"Ya mean from here?" he asked.

"Yes."

"Not that I know of. 'Course there might be. I'm not on top of things like I used to be, ya know. What's in Brodhead?"

"I don't know," said Steel. "Where's a good place in town to get breakfast?"

"Try Emma's. About a block down."

"Thanks," said Steel.

As Steel was walking out, the old man said, "So you think the boy did these things?"

"I don't know," said Steel.

"A real shame," Steel heard him say. "A real shame."

# Chapter 19

"We have a problem," said Donofrio. The call had been to Clyde.

"Willie got his ass kicked by this guy named Steel," said Angelo Donofrio to his regular receptionist and bodyguard, Clyde. "Your cousin was totally useless."

Clyde had come to the office as soon as he had been summoned by Donofrio. Willie was still woozy when Clyde arrived. "Gee, I'm sorry, Mr. Donofrio," said Clyde. Aside, to his cousin, he said, "Come on. Can you walk? I'll take you to the hospital." Clyde kept looking over his shoulder at Donofrio, afraid not to.

"After you get rid of that tub of lard," said Donofrio, "get somebody to clean up the blood on the rug."

"Yes, Mr. Donofrio," said Clyde.

"Before you leave, get Mex on the phone. Leave a message for him or whatever it is you do," said Donofrio.

"Sure thing, Mr. Donofrio," said Clyde.

Willie still wobbled when he tried to stand on his own. Willie and Clyde were about the same height, but Clyde looked trimmer. He wasn't smaller; he had the same girth, just more muscle.

"I left the message for Mex, just as you instructed, Mr. Donofrio. He should call in soon. Okay if I take my cousin to the emergency room now?" asked Clyde.

"Just leave him there," said Donofrio. "I want your ass back here quick."

The phone rang as Willie and Clyde were leaving. Donofrio grabbed it on the first ring.

"Talk," said Donofrio.

"It's me, boss. Mex."

"I told you not to call me boss."

After a pause, "Hokay - Mr. Donofrio."

"Can you get a hold of Thumbs?" asked Donofrio.

"Sure. No problem. I get a hold o' him now."

"I want to see both of you in my office in one hour," said Donofrio. "I have a job for you - and some questions."

"Hokay. We both be there."

Donofrio slammed down the phone .

After Mex was sure the line was dead, he said, "Fuck you. Gringo ass hole."

# Chapter 20

Brad Kendall was lucky enough to find a restaurant in Brodhead that needed a dishwasher. The job provided a place to sleep in a partitioned section at the rear of the building as an added bonus. The room appeared to have been slept in by different people at different times. The aroma of the cubicle was of fried food and sweat. But it was warm, dry, and free, and Brad was glad to get it.

He had allowed his facial hair to grow freely and the makings of a beard began to appear. Though it was a bit unruly now, in time, he knew he would shape it. Brad had always thought he would like a beard, and now it was not only possible, it was expedient, anything to blur his features so as to avoid detection.

A week had passed since his arrival in Brodhead and he considered himself fortunate that he'd picked, though strictly by chance, a quiet, out of the way, place. He never thought he would be satisfied to just do his dishes and go to his room.

He'd told the owner that his mom and dad had split-up and were contemplating a divorce and that he had to drop out of school. Both parents had found someone else and he didn't feel welcome at either of their homes.

The owner, a Greek immigrant, whose name was Nick, spoke English reasonably well and Brad surmised he'd been in the United States for awhile. Nick and Brad had a lengthy conversation during his interview for the dishwasher job. Nick must have figured Brad could do the job, or maybe he just felt sorry for him.

Brad felt guilt about lying to Nick but had no choice but to give him a phony name, Brent Kolar. Brad was becoming adept at lying, something he'd never done before or had any reason to. Brad figured if he did his job, didn't steal, or hurt anybody, that it might be okay. Circumstances dictated his concealment.

After a week had gone by, Brad called his parents from a pay phone in town. He lied to them about taking a bus out of town. He accidentally told them where he was and found himself deceiving them by telling them he was leaving. He had no idea where else to go, and Brodhead was as good a place as any, so he stayed.

He'd sent Sibby a post card but didn't put a return address on it. As he thought about it now, his message seemed so feeble under the circumstances, and he wished he hadn't sent it.

He missed his parents and his home, but mostly he missed Sibby and yearned to be with her. He wanted to hold her and tell her how sorry he was for everything that had come to pass.

The news of the murders had followed him to Wisconsin, but little was said in the Brodhead newspaper. He would find copies of the Milwaukee papers left in the restaurant. Gradually, the story went from page three to page ten and page twenty-three, until it was gone.

Numerous articles appeared showing him spotted in Murray, Kentucky, Brainerd, Minnesota, and even San Jose, California. The early reports showed a high school picture of him. Later, only his name was mentioned. Finally, he became a ghost, unseen by anyone.

After a month, he began to feel safer. He was still cautious, but he stopped looking over his shoulder as often.

In the mirror, he saw a stranger, a brown-haired man with long hair and a beard. His sideburns had faded as his hairline blended into his facial hair. He thought he had to begun to resemble the wolf man, someone he'd seen in 1940s movies.

Brad Kendall had become Brent Kolar, dishwasher and hermit. In his spare-time, he watched the twelve-inch black and white TV Nick had provided for him. Brad bought himself an inexpensive radio with earplugs at the corner drug store so he could listen to music during the night, when everyone else was asleep, and he wasn't, because he couldn't, due to the demons in his mind who came to haunt him.

Brad had no identification as Brent Kolar. No one, not even Nick, asked for any. Nick paid him cash so no paperwork was processed. Brad stayed in his room and rarely wandered outside his confines, except in the evening, when it was dark, and he felt the good people of Brodhead would not see him.

The time would come, he knew, that someone would recognize him. Identification papers showing the new name would be vital. He had no idea how to acquire fake Ids but he knew he would have to learn.

Brad shuddered at how quickly he had become a liar, a cheat, and a murder suspect. It scared him at how much he had been able to alter his physical appearance; It frightened him more how much the core of him had changed.

# Chapter 21

Luis Smith had long ago changed the name he had been born with in Mexico to his new American name. He was Smith, as American as he could be. He earned a good income and drove a nice car. He worked for Angelo Donofrio. *Mr.* Donofrio - the *Prick*, he thought. But the *Prick* paid well, and if Luis did his job well, *Mr.* Donofrio left him alone.

*Mr.* Donofrio called him Mex. Luis didn't like that. He wanted to be called Luis. Better yet, he wanted to be called *Mr.* Smith.

The last job Luis did for Mr. Donofrio got botched. It wasn't Luis' fault. He was sent to do a job and he was doing it when that big Gringo came in, the kid, the one they called Kendall. The kid messed everything up. Luis had to hastily leave his mission; he had to escape out the window. Luis didn't like to go through windows

127

anymore, though he'd done it for years. He preferred to use the door. That's what doors are for, to walk through. Not windows. But he had no choice. He had to get out through the window even though he walked in the front door.

This was a sloppy job. The stupid kid walked right in the door Luis himself had left open. Luis had done sloppy jobs in the past but he hadn't messed one up in a long time. So even though it wasn't his fault, he ended up going out the window. Lucky for him, the snow that night covered his tracks. Lucky for him, the big kid got blamed.

Now Mr. Donofrio says somebody named Steel is nosing around. After he talked to Mr. Donofrio on the phone, Luis had to get Thumbs. He doesn't like to be called Thumbs. His name is Luther Smith. So Luis and Luther are both Smith. Luis is Mexican and thinks he's an American because his name is Smith, while Luther, an African-American, is called Smith because his mother didn't know who his father was. Mr. Donofrio refers to Luther as Thumbs because he has a thumb missing on his left hand.

Luis and Luther Smith got their reprimands and new instructions from Donofrio in his office. Donofrio made both of them nervous. Luther kept his hands in his pockets the whole time. Luis toyed with the scar on his throat. When he caught himself, he stopped, but his fingers kept finding their way back.

Luis and Luther, Mex and Thumbs, could easily have done away with their employer. But they would have killed their golden goose, their conduit to cash. So they tolerated Donofrio and offered false respect.

They left Donofrio's office with their directive and mission statement. This was, after all, a business they were in, a serious business, a deadly business, and they were professional businessmen.

"Kill Steel." They knew what to do.

This was the part of their job description duties that most appealed to them.

# Chapter 22

There was nothing more for him in Eagle Lake, so after he ate lunch at Emma's Restaurant, Steel headed for Brodhead. In an hour or two he would be there. He'd called from the restaurant and Mike Collins had informed him that Sibby Rockwald had been moved from her Uncle's house to McHenry County and was welcomed by the Hessmullers. Gus and Emily were concerned that Scrap Iron, Steel's dog, would resent her. On the contrary, he took to Sibby, and acted as if he belonged to her. *Scrap Iron was a sap for a pretty face,* thought Steel, as his mind wandered across the meandering miles.

Steel pulled into Brodhead about three. He knew he was in the downtown section but there wasn't much to it. He'd seen signs on the way informing him where to buy cheese. He hadn't seen a cheese house anywhere. He expected more from the town, but no matter, he didn't come for cheese. He came to get leads on Brad Kendall, who he assumed had left town weeks ago.

Steel knew why he came to Brodhead but he wasn't convinced this was the best way to find Brad Kendall. He'd grown tired of talking to everyone about the boy and decided it was time he talked to the boy himself. He was determined to discover his destination.

Steel surveyed the entire downtown area from where he stood. He could see the post office, the police station, a drug store, a hardware store, a grocery store, a restaurant, a real estate and insurance office, and a barber shop.

He headed for the police station.

# Chapter 23

When the two plainclothes detectives arrived to pick up Sibby Rockwald, she was cautious as Steel had advised. She insisted the men slip their identification under the door and when their billfolds couldn't squeeze under the tight opening, they had to remove the cards. The IDs showed their photos so Sibby was able to eye the men through the opening of the chain-latched door.

Satisfied, she returned their identification, retrieved the bag she had packed earlier, and joined the men outside the door. One of the detectives offered to carry the bag but she insisted on carrying it herself. She'd told her aunt that she was leaving under protective custody, and as Justin Steel had directed her, Sibby didn't divulge her destination. She didn't know herself exactly where she was headed. Her aunt touched her on the shoulder, but didn't attempt to stop Sibby.

An hour and a half later, Sibby and the two men were sitting at the gated entrance to Steel's property. Gus Hessmuller met them at the gate after Emily had spoken with them through the intercom. The big dog was with Gus in the pickup truck front seat but when Gus left the truck to unlock the gate, he left Scrap Iron behind in the vehicle. The dog sat at attention.

Sibby observed from the back seat of the black Dodge Intrepid and witnessed the proceedings with interest. After her long drive, she still wasn't sure where she was, thinking they might be entering a forest preserve. The Intrepid followed the pickup for a full minute as the dirt road wound its way to the house.

The guards escorted Sibby into the house and once they were satisfied the inside was safe, the men returned to the Intrepid and watched from outside the residence but well inside the property fence line.

After the detectives were inside their vehicle, Gus released Scrap Iron from the truck cab. The dog ran to the Intrepid, circled it, then followed Gus into the house.

When Sibby entered the house, Emily immediately hugged her. This caught Sibby off-guard and she melted in the woman's arms. After a quick tour of the house interior, Emily showed Sibby to the bedroom that would be hers.

Sibby didn't want to be alone so she joined Emily in the kitchen for cookies and milk. Gus was restraining Scrap Iron on a leash, not sure how the dog would react to Sibby, a stranger in the house.

When Sibby saw Scrap Iron watching her, she went to her knees on the kitchen floor and motioned for the dog to come. Gus looked to Emily for guidance and she just shrugged. Reluctantly, Gus unchained the dog and it ran toward Sibby.

A moment later, she and the dog played as she tried to hug him while he bobbed and weaved and licked her face. She laughed and the dog let out a loud bark that set Sibby back a bit, but they resumed their parrying.

"What's his name?" asked Sibby.

"Scrap Iron," said Gus.

"What a neat name," she said.

# Chapter 24

"How could you let her leave?" bellowed a now sober Frank Rockwald.

"It's not like I had a choice," said Kathy, his wife. "She made up her own mind. She's probably safer where the police took here. After your big mouth about Richard and me, how could she stay with me? You were no bargain in your drunken state either."

"But we're her family," objected Frank. "She belongs with us."

"Does she? In this house? . . . You hated her father. I slept with him. I'm not even sure *we* belong together. Wherever she is, she has to be better off."

"You slut," he barked. "What gives you the right to decide where *my* niece is better off?"

She reached back to slap him but he grabbed her hand in the middle of her swing. He acted as if he wanted to hit her. He put his hand up and then checked himself. He did want to hit her but realized it wasn't the right thing to do. He wasn't sure if he loved her anymore. He certainly felt different about her, but he knew he couldn't and shouldn't strike her.

"Go ahead and hit me," she screamed. "You know you want to hit me, so go ahead."

"Go away," he said. "Just leave me alone."

"You started this with your bellowing and name calling," she said. "Now you decide you want to stop." She continued her badgering. He had riled her and she wasn't ready to stop.

He placed his head in his hands. His head hurt from the liquor he had earlier and its effects were wearing off and were being replaced with a headache. He no longer respected his wife but he regretted calling her a slut. He felt guilty about his brother's death and about its effects on Sibby and how he couldn't take care of her properly. He was neglecting his business and his clients. He had pressed so hard into his head and eyes that when he removed his hands, his eyes saw spots as they tried to focus.

"Your brother was twice the man you ever were," she ranted. Spittle dribbled over her lips. "When you could get it up, it wasn't worth fussing over. You're not a man . . . you're a worm."

"Enough already," he said, abruptly cutting off her tirade.

"I've got more to say," she continued.

"He's dead, Kathy. And I'm glad. Our marriage is dead, too."

"You're the one who should be dead," she said. "Richard should be alive and you should be dead."

"I'm responsible for Richard's death," he said softly.

The understated manner in which Frank declared the fact jolted Kathy into calm. She stuttered as she spoke. "*You* killed Richard?" The words she spoke to her husband hung in the air.

"No," he said. "I didn't kill him but I'm as responsible as if I had."

"I don't understand," she murmured.

He stared at the blank wall in front of him, then turned to his wife. "He owed money to some disreputable people. I helped Richard borrow money from these vultures. Richard didn't repay them on time. These people were angry at me. I thought they might kill me - or you. I think Richard transferred the money out of the country through his export business. I think he could have repaid his loan but he thought he was smarter than everybody else. Actually, he was the stupid one. Richard must have thought they were just going to walk away and let him keep the money. I don't know what he was thinking but it got him and his family killed and I knew it was going to happen, that they were going to kill him, and I didn't warn him, or try to stop them, as if I could. I was angry with him and I was glad he was finally going to get what was coming to him. That's why I'm so sick over it all now. His wife and kids died, and I could have stopped it. I'm responsible, God help me."

Kathy sat silent looking at her husband and wondered how their life had come to this moment. Frank was having the same thought.

Their reverie was interrupted by a fierce pounding on the front door.

# Chapter 25

Justin Steel entered the Brodhead police station. There wasn't much to it, three desks and a rear office. Luckily the police chief was in so he escorted Steel to the office.

"Did you receive the phone call from Mike Collins in Illinois?" asked Steel.

"Yes," said the young, slender police chief, named Haskell. "But frankly, I wasn't impressed."

"I'm sure he wasn't trying to impress you," said Steel, as he smiled to himself.

"You have no jurisdiction here, Mr. Steel."

"I realize that. I'm working privately at the request of the jurisdictional authorities. I want to help locate Brad Kendall, who is wanted to answer some questions."

"What makes you think he's here?"

"We believe he was here but we don't believe he's here now," said Steel. He was trying very hard not to

141

antagonize the youthful local authority who obviously felt threatened by outside interference, probably because of his age and lack of experience.

"He's not here," said Chief Haskell.

"What makes you so certain?" said Steel, not willing to let Haskell get away with his uninformed statement.

"It's my town; I get paid to know," he said, defiantly.

Steel let his comment pass. "Is it all right to look around and ask some questions in case somebody might remember him?"

"Nobody will remember him," said Haskell.

"I see," said Steel, getting inwardly irritated, but trying not to show it. "So it can't hurt if I just ask around?"

"I don't want you bothering my people."

*This guy is a piece of work*, thought Steel. "I'll be discreet."

"I don't like you Mr. Steel. Guys like you are scavengers on the justice system. But you obviously have friends in high places. Go ahead, ask your questions. One complaint and you're finished. Understand?"

"Yes. Thanks," said Steel. He stood up and immediately left the unfriendly atmosphere of the office. The sooner he got done in this town, the happier he'd be, was the way he figured.

He stepped out into the brisk winter cold. A chill ran through him. He tried to shake it off as he headed for the post office. Crossing the street, he fought the glare of the tepid sun that hung low in the seasonal sky.

Stepping into the building was like walking into a spa. It was a small edifice and two teller's windows faced him. One window was closed. The other was tended by a man about sixty. He had thick glasses and a warm smile. His crooked teeth didn't diminish his pleasant face.

"Help you?" he asked.

Steel produced his business card and a picture of Brad Kendall. A postal patron could walk in at any time so Steel got right down to business, while he could.

"Ever see him?" asked Steel.

"Nope," said the clerk.

"Look again."

He adjusted his glasses and came within six inches of the picture. "Nope," he repeated.

"You ever run across the name, Brad Kendall?" Steel was thinking that if Kendall received any mail, this was the man who might have seen it. He probably saw every piece of mail that that this town received in the past forty years. He thought awhile. He sort of stared into space as if thinking was a process separate from everyday living. "Nope."

"You sure?"

"Yep."

"Thanks," said Steel.

"Sure," said the single syllable public servant.

Steel stepped back out into the cold street. He'd hoped to learn more with his visit. No reason to visit the real estate office. It wasn't likely Kendall bought a house. More possibly, Kendall may have stopped into the hardware store or the drug store.

The most likely remaining choice was the restaurant. Maybe Kendall stopped to eat. Steel realized he was hungry himself so he walked about a block until he came to Nick's Restaurant.

# Chapter 26

"You sure he lives here?" said Luther Smith, also known as Thumbs.

"Yeah. Sure. He's home. I see his car," said Luis Smith, Mex.

Smith and Smith  making a house call, not real brothers, but brothers in crime, brothers in blood, other people's blood. Luis pounded on the front door again.

Neither Frank or Kathy responded. Kathy stood up and went to the bathroom, wiping her eyes as she did. Frank adjusted his shirt into his pants and walked to the front door where the pounding was occurring.

"Who is it?" asked Frank.

No one answered. Frank walked to a side window where he could get a better view of the front porch. He saw two men: one tall, one short; one African-American, one Hispanic. Frank recognized the short one from Donofrio's office. *Not good*, he thought.

The pounding continued.

"Open da fuckin' door," said Luis. "It's cold out here."

Frank obeyed and opened the door, though not sure why. He was concerned, but not afraid, since he recognized one of them.

"What do you want?" asked Frank.

They walked past him into the living room. They didn't seem interested in answering his question. They split up and inspected all the rooms. One door was locked.

"What's in here?" asked Luther.

"The bathroom," said Frank.

"Open it," said Luther.

"It's occupied," said Frank.

"I don't give a fuck," said Luther.

"My wife's in there."

"Open it now, ass hole."

"Honey, please come out," said Frank. His concern was turning into fear.

"Go away. Leave me alone," she said.

"Shit," said Luther, as he pushed the door in with his shoulder.

The door frame splintered as the door opened easily. She was sitting down and tried to cover herself.

"Get up, bitch," said Luther.

"What's wrong with you people?" said Frank, as he attempted to get past Luther so he could close the door.

"Shut the fuck up," said Luther, as he shoved his open hand into Frank's face. Frank flew backwards, like a wobbly mannequin, crashed into a hallway wall, and slid down into a crumpled heap.

During the melee, Kathy quickly dressed herself. She tried to come to her husband's aid, but Luther easily held her back. "Frank, Frank - my God, you've killed him," she screamed.

Luis watched with delight and laughed aloud. But he didn't like hysterical women, so he said to Luther, "Shut the fuckin' cunt up."

"Put a sock in it, bitch," said Luther.

But she continued, "You've killed Frank."

Luis assumed Frank was just out cold, so he nudged his limp body. But after Luis kicked the body and got no response, he put his fingers on Frank's carotid artery. There was no sign of life. He wasn't supposed to die. It was just a love tap.

"Chit," said Luis, as he looked up to Luther.

Kathy kept screaming, "You've killed him." Her shrill sound in close quarters reverberated off the walls.

Luther grabbed her right hand and put his Smith & Wesson .38 in it. He placed her finger on the trigger, holding her and guiding her all the while. She was like a doll in his powerful hands, without a will of her own. Luther edged her toward Frank's body.

When they were inches from Frank's head, he pressed her finger to squeeze the trigger. The deafening blast resounded in the confined area and in the process obliterated Frank's face, splattering blood in Kathy's unbelieving eyes.

Kathy mewed in her stupor and didn't even realize that Luther's gloved hand had taken the revolver from her hand. Luis grasped her shoulders and shook her back to the grizzly reality.

"Look a' me beetch," said Luis. She looked at him, looking but not seeing. "Where is da girl?"

"They took her," she managed.

"Who took her?" asked Luis.

"The police," she said.

Luis looked to Luther, then back to Kathy, whom he still held in his hands. She was oblivious to his grasp. Perhaps he kept her from collapsing. "Where dey take her?" he asked.

"To Steel's house," she said.

"Where is dat?"

"I don't know."

He slapped her, but gently. He didn't want to knock her into unconsciousness or kill her. He wanted to scare her into giving him information.

"Where is dis Steel place?" He demanded.

"All I have is phone number," she said. A trickle of blood ran from her nose and blended with Frank's splattered blood on her face.

"What is the number, beetch," said Luis.

She pointed to a book case. A business card with a phone number written on it was visible. Luis gave Kathy to Luther and located a telephone in the living room. He dialed the number on the card.

He heard a recorded message from a female with a monotone voice. In essence, it said the phone was outside the calling range and to try later.

"Las' chance, muchacha," said Luis. "Where is Steel?"

"I don't know," she said.

"Kill her," said Luis.

"No, please," she pleaded.

148

Luther took her hand again, placed the revolver in it, and put the piece in her mouth. Her eyes were wide open as she watched him standing directly in front of her. She was starting to gag when the blast went off. She dropped to the floor, her eyes still wide open, her finger still on the trigger, the gun still in her hand.

"Les' go," said Luis.
They left the gun. They had others.

# Chapter 27

The aroma of food hit Steel straight on as he entered Nick's Restaurant. The door had old-fashioned bells above it and they tinkled as he walked through, attracting his attention to them. The first smell he identified as hamburger frying on a grill with sautéed onions and mushrooms. Freshly brewed coffee accompanied the first scent.

Many patrons filled the restaurant on the midwinter, late-afternoon. About fifteen tables covered with red and white table cloths augmented the main counter that seated a dozen. All the tables were occupied but only half the counter seats were filled. Steel took a spot near the center of the counter.

No one seemed to notice when he walked in. It was better that way since he had no desire to draw attention to himself.

A blonde-haired, rotund waitress with a pretty face approached him with a coffee pot and poured into a cup that was already placed in front of him. He could have stopped her from pouring but it smelled too good not to have any. She placed a menu before him and promised to return. Steel realized he had passed a coat rack near the entrance so he went back and hung-up his top coat and scarf. When he returned the waitress was waiting for him to order.

"A cheeseburger with grilled onions," he said. "And fries."

"If you order deluxe, it comes with slaw," she said.

"Good. That's what I want," he said. He enjoyed indulging his whims when he was on the road. He was tired of his regimented home cooking.

"You want to order dessert now, or later," she said. Her smile was contagious. He smiled back.

"What's good?" he asked.

"Pie," she said.

"What kind you got?"

"Cherry, or cherry," she laughed.

"I'll have the cherry," he said.

"Good choice," she smiled again and took her menu back, the one Steel never opened.

He loosened his tie, relaxed, and sipped his coffee. The drive and the cold outdoors had tired him but the beverage was invigorating. As he waited for his burger he noticed his reflection in the mirror on the wall facing him. His image made him feel self-conscious. He tried to ignore it, but it kept looking back at him.

When his cheeseburger was set before him, he poured ketchup on the fries and began eating, momentarily forgetting the mirror. After a while, he was back looking at himself. *What a dumb idea,* he thought. He could think of two reasons why the mirror was placed there. It made the room seem bigger, as if people could be that easily fooled. A waitress could see if someone sat down at the counter or needed service. *Just turn around,* Steel figured. Meanwhile, he continued to watch himself. He tried to see if, in the reflection, anyone else was watching him, but he couldn't tell.

The waitress brought the pie just as he finished the burger. *The mirror must work,* he thought. She refilled his coffee cup and removed his empty platter. After his second bite into the pie, he encountered a cherry pit. Thereafter, he ate more carefully.

When she came to remove the pie plate, she tried to fill his cup again, but he stopped her.

"Fresh cherries in the pie, weren't they?" he said.

"Fresh out of the can," she said.

"I had a pit in the cherries, I just thought . . ."

"Pit's fresh out of the can, too," she laughed.

"What's your name - if I may ask?" said Steel.

"Maggie. Why? You going to ask me out?"

It took him a moment to realize she was joking. "Sure," he said. "Let's go."

"Can I bring my six kids?" she said.

"The more the merrier." Steel went along with the buffoonery.

"How about my husband?"

"That's where I draw the line," he said.

"Sorry. If my hubby can't come with, I can't either." They laughed together. It felt good for Steel to laugh.

Steel suddenly remembered why he was there. He produced a four-by-six head shot of Brad Kendall. "You ever see him?"

"Are you a cop?" She seemed to have taken a step back and her smile was gone.

"Private," he said, as he produced a business card and placed it next to the photo, so she could see them both easily. She craned her neck but didn't come any closer.

"Why? What's he done?"

"I just want to talk to him," said Steel.

"Hold on," she said. She called out toward the cooking area in back. "Nick, come out here a minute."

Throughout the restaurant, heads turned. It became noticeably quieter.

"What's the problem?" said the small man, called Nick.

"Look at that picture," she said.

"You know him?" asked Steel.

"Why?" asked Nick.

"I'm trying to find him for his mother and father," said Steel. It was only a half-truth, but it was better than a lie.

Steel didn't get the sympathetic, cooperative response he'd hoped for. "I don't know him. Now, get out of my place," said Nick.

"I was just finishing my coffee," said Steel. It was obvious, Nick and Maggie recognized the photo but Steel didn't want to create a ruckus. Everybody in the restaurant was now staring at them and Steel felt it would be better if he came back when it was less crowded, whenever that would be.

"Okay. You finish you coffee, then you go," said Nick. Steel noticed that Nick's Greek accent became more prominent as he became excited.

154

Nick was irate and Steel didn't know why. Maggie wasn't smiling anymore and a look of concern was on her face. Steel was glad he ate first, before he produced the photo. The people of Brodhead could be nice, he surmised, but at this moment, he'd hit a nerve, and they felt threatened.

Steel put two tens on the counter. One easily covered his tab. The second ten he placed under his coffee cup. While he was putting on his coat, he saw her pocketing the tip.

Steel waved to her as he was walking out of the restaurant. She started to raise her hand to wave back but checked herself. The customers returned to their food.

Steel stepped out into the cold street.

# Chapter 28

Mex and Thumbs called Donofrio from their car phone after they'd distanced themselves from Frank and Kathy Rockwald. Smith and Smith were someplace on Green Bay Road. Luther was driving and Luis had the phone.

"It was a accident, Mr. Donofrio. We was just gonna talk."

"Accidents seem to follow you two buffoons around. I thought I was working with professionals," said Donofrio.

"We took care of it," said Luis.

"Is it clean? Can anyone connect you?" asked Donofrio.

"Is clean," said Luis. "We was never there."

"But it won't be long before somebody puts the pieces together," said Donofrio. "Too many Rockwalds are dying. It'll come back on us."

"No way, Boss," said Luis. "We is pros."

"My name to you is Mr. Donofrio. Not boss."

"Yeah, Mr. Donofrio," said Luis. He wanted to tell him to go fuck himself. He had a name, too. It was Mr. Smith. Not Mex.

"So, you're a pro. Ha!" laughed Donofrio. "Our good friend, Steel, is somebody you know from way back. Do you remember Marshall Brisby? Somebody you said you took care of about a dozen years ago. Remember, Mex? He's Steel. Brisby is Steel."

Luther Smith made a left turn. He was lost. He was trying to locate Route 41. Everything looked alike to him in this neighborhood.

Luis continued conversing with Donofrio. "Who da fuck is Brisby?"

"Think, Mex. The accountant in the fire. Another job you apparently botched. I thought you guys were good."

"Brisby?" said Mex. "Brisby's dead. He was a fuckin' woos. We left him to burn."

"If Brisby is Steel, he's no pushover," said Donofrio. "Trust me on that."

"Fuckin' Brisby is Steel? No shit?" said Luis. "I remamber tha' cock sucker. He woke up when we was lookin' aroun'. I remember. We croaked his fuckin' ol' lady."

"And his kids, too," added Donofrio.

"I want this Steel, or Brisby, or wha'ever his fuckin' name is," said Luis.

"That's why I sent you out. To get Steel. I have an address for you. Do I have to do all your work for you?" said Donofrio.

158

Luis wrote it down on the back of a racing form that was on the seat between Luther and himself. "Where da fuck is this place?" said Luis.

"Get a map, Mex," said Donofrio.

"Don't worry, boss. I find it and this time, the fucker's dead, for sure."

Donofrio was tired of correcting the ignorant Mexican. He was thinking perhaps Steel might perform a fine service if he killed Mex and Thumbs. Either way, Steel, or them, was okay.

"Good luck, Mex," said Donofrio.

After they hung up, Luis said, "ass hole," into the dead instrument.

He looked to Luther and said, "I got some good news and I got some bad news, about Steel."

After Donofrio hung up, he was ambivalent about Mex and Thumbs. Earlier, he'd received word from upstairs. The FBI was sniffing around. It was time to close up shop. He had passports for himself and Clyde, his bodyguard. Along the way, he would feed Clyde to the fishes. Then he would go alone where no one would find him.

# Chapter 29

Daylight was nearly gone. The sun had done all it could but its warmth couldn't reach the cold main streets of Brodhead, Wisconsin.

Since it would soon be dark and Steel hadn't finished his business in the town, he decided to find a place to spend the night. He wasn't sure where to begin looking.

The second man on the street that Steel casually encountered informed him there was a small motel about six blocks west of town. Steel drove the impoverished road for over a mile before he spotted a sign that read *Bailey's Lodge*. A smaller sign hung below announced there were indeed vacancies.

When Steel entered the tiny registration office, an affable middle-aged man told him how fortunate he was to get the last room. Since Steel had seen no other cars in the parking lot, he assumed the clerk told this to everyone. He paid for one night but told the man behind the counter he wasn't certain how long he would have to stay.

The room, one of eight in the one-story row building, was cozy. It had a full-sized bed, ample for Steel. It also contained a compact desk, two wooden chairs, a television set, and a telephone.

Steel carried in one bag. It was all he needed for the night. The trunk still contained the two file boxes of information he was carting around. They would be safe enough to leave in the car overnight as would his extra clothes. He brought in his firearms just in case he needed them. A better reason is he wouldn't want to explain their theft to the police should an unexpected break-in occur. The area looked safe enough and open hostility didn't appear likely.

He determined he would not venture out tonight. Tomorrow he would try Nick again. Steel was sure Nick had seen the boy but a month had elapsed since the postcard to Sibby, so one more day wouldn't matter. Besides, he would have to eat breakfast somewhere and Nick's place seemed to be the only place in town. He thought he should eat before asking questions or he wouldn't get the chance if today was any indication.

After changing into lounging clothes, he went to the phone. The first call was to Mike Collins. Steel got him on his car phone as he traveled home from his office, in rush hour traffic again. Mike had nothing new so Steel told him he might have a lead. He also gave Mike the motel telephone number.

He next phoned the Hessmullers. Emily answered. Sibby and Scrap Iron were getting attached, she told him. Steel was glad for Sibby and the dog. Everything was fine, Emily said, and not to worry.

Steel hoped Nick would talk with him tomorrow so he could, for better or worse, find and bring Brad Kendall home, to the authorities, to his parents, and to face Sibby.

# Chapter 30

Brent Kolar, really Brad Kendall, was in the back room, behind the kitchen, when Justin Steel sat down at the counter at Nick's Restaurant. But when Maggie summoned Nick to the floor, Brad was entering the kitchen to start on the current batch of dirty dishes. He saw Nick talking to the stranger at the counter, and though he didn't know who the man was, or hear what was being said, he watched as the stranger showed Nick a photo and thought he heard his name, Brad Kendall, a name he had all but forgotten himself.

Brad wished this day had never come but he knew that one day it would. Brad knew what he must do. Without hesitation, he stripped off his apron, put on his coat, and grabbed his always ready duffel bag. At the last instant, he threw his radio into it.

The key to Nick's old pickup truck hung on a peg hook in the hallway near the rear door. Brad took the key and replaced it with a sealed envelope with Nick's name written on it and pressed it onto the peg hook until it broke through the paper envelope and conspicuously hung there for Nick to find. The note inside had been written weeks ago and was in Brad's bag, ready for just this occasion.

When he started the truck, it sounded louder than usual. He also knew if he didn't warm it up enough, it could sputter and die out. But he grew impatient and as he drove away, he hoped it would keep going. The gas gauge showed the tank was one-third full but he couldn't stop for gas now.

He headed for Route 11, which would take him through Monroe, and the rest of the southern end of Wisconsin. His plan was to reach Dubuque, Iowa. After that, he had no plans. He was in flight and he was afraid, again. He was fleeing for his life. They were after him, again. No - some man was after him. He pressed harder on the accelerator.

Nick cried as he read the note Brad left him. He wasn't Brent Kolar; he was Brad Kendall. His parents weren't divorced; they were still married. He, Brad Kendall, was wanted for questioning about a multiple murder. Worse yet, he was the primary suspect, probably the only suspect.

Brad thanked Nick for all he had done for him and wished he could have stayed forever. He was sorry he took his truck and he would leave it somewhere safe where it could be retrieved.

166

Brad asked one more favor. Wait before calling the police; give him a head start. He ended the letter with the words, "with true affection from your friend."

# Chapter 31

When Justin Steel entered Nick's Restaurant, Chief Haskell and one of his deputies were talking with Nick at one of the back tables. The Chief motioned for Steel to come over.

"You were right, Mr. Steel," said Haskell. "Nick discovered his truck missing this morning. The guy who worked here as a dishwasher appears to have taken it. Nick said the boy is the one you showed him a picture of."

"Did he leave a note or anything?" asked Steel.

"No, he just stole the truck and took off," said Haskell.

"Can I ask Nick some questions?" asked Steel.

Chief Haskell looked at Nick. Nick didn't say anything. Haskell looked back to Steel. "Sure, go ahead."

"Nick, when did Brad Kendall come to work for you?" asked Steel.

Nick looked puzzled. "Oh, you mean Brent. I forgot his name isn't Brent. He came about two weeks before Christmas. The other dishwasher joined the Army and I needed somebody quick. Brent - I mean Brad saw my sign in the window. He was a good worker, polite. He kept to himself, quiet. I liked him - and trusted him, too."

"Aren't you angry he stole your truck?" asked Steel.

"If he needed it, it's okay."

"Aren't you worried about getting it back?"

"It was old, about fifteen years. I buy it used," he said, slipping into his slight Greek accent.

As Steel questioned Nick, Chief Haskell excused himself to take a phone call. Within minutes, he returned.

"They recovered the truck," said Haskell. "It was abandoned on Route 11 near Browntown, not too far out of Monroe. The trooper said it has a flat but is otherwise undamaged."

"Any sign of Kendall?" asked Steel.

"No. Nothing. They're looking around but he could be out of state by now," said Haskell.

Steel noticed Nick had a minuscule smile on his face. Nick tried to conceal it but not until Steel already spotted it. Haskell was more worried about the truck, thought Steel, than he was about Kendall.

Steel took Nick to the side. "You're covering for him, aren't you?" said Steel.

Nick didn't reply.

"I have to bring him to Illinois to clear him - or to convict him," said Steel. "I don't want to see him hurt. I

170

promised his parents I would bring him home safely. If you care about the boy, you'll be honest with me, and at the same time, keep yourself out of trouble in case the boy is guilty."

Nick's eyes widened. "I don't need no trouble. I just feel sorry for him. I don't know where he is." Nick looked sad and Steel believed what he said.

Steel approached Chief Haskell. "I'd like to go after him," said Steel. "Could you call ahead to whoever is in charge in that neck of the woods and tell them who I am?"

"I can do that," said Haskell. "But I can't promise any better of a reception than you got from me. By the way, who *are you really*, Mr. Steel?"

# Chapter 32

Brad Kendall saw no open gas stations along the way as he desperately tried to separate himself from Brodhead. Even in Monroe, every station was closed by five, once it was already dark. There must be one open, he thought, but he wasn't finding it. He continued driving, very concerned about running out of fuel when the rear tire blew. It happened suddenly, like a gunshot, or what he thought a gunshot would sound like. He pulled the truck off the road onto the apron once he realized what had occurred and was relieved that he was able to do so without further mishap.

He searched the bed of the truck but there was no spare or jack under the canvas tarpaulin covering. He was stuck in the middle of nowhere, and it was dark and it was cold so he retreated to the cab to ponder over what he should do next. He had no panic but neither could he come up with an alternative solution to his dilemma. As his eyes adjusted to the darkness, and it was extremely dark now that he'd shut off the headlights, he noticed a road sign about fifty feet ahead of him. In black on white, it read, Browntown, two miles.

"Shit," he said. "What else can go wrong?" He said it aloud, but only he heard it.

He rifled through his duffel bag and luckily he'd packed a cap and some gloves. He retied his sneakers and bundled himself as well as he could. He re-zipped his bag and got out. He headed for Browntown by foot. No cars passed from either direction. He hadn't decided if this was good or bad.

It was nearly seven and it had been dark for about two hours. He hadn't actually been driving all this time. About halfway between Brodhead and Monroe, he'd parked for about an hour, as he tried to calm himself, as he wondered if he was doing the right thing, running away - to nowhere. He decided then that he had no choice but to keep going.

Now, as he walked, trying to stay warm, focusing on his steps in the dark, listening to the rhythmic crunch of each step, he wondered if any animals were watching him from the darkness of the wooded area. A city boy in the wilderness is who he was at the moment, and he was terrified of the blackness around him. In the urban surroundings of his home in Illinois there were periodic street lights, passing cars, familiar room-lit homes. Here, there was nothing, at least nothing he could see or conceptualize.

He trudged on. Brittle twigs, dry leaves, and road gravel crunched under his steps. It hadn't snowed in days, but occasional slippery spots threatened his footing.

After a while, the hike became invigorating. After all, it was only two miles. He used to run that much each day just to keep in shape for football. That time seemed so long ago, as if he were thinking about someone else.

His thoughts began to focus on things he missed and lost, things that could never be the same again. Christmas had come and gone. He thought of it now as he had thought of it on Christmas Eve, when he sat alone in his room at the restaurant and listened to Christmas songs on the radio until he eventually fell asleep.

He ached now as he ached that night. The loss of everything. He missed his mom and dad. They had been so good to him and he had hurt them so badly.

He thought of Sibby as he trod on in the dark, and how painful it must be for her to go on without her family. Brad lamented for her, and for himself, and for his loss of her, and how he knew they could never be together again.

Why had he run? Because he was afraid? Yes. Because he was guilty? No. He could not have done such a thing. How terrible for those poor people, her mom and dad, and Richie and Cindy. How terrible for Sibby. How he wanted to comfort her that night. But she had already made it clear that she wanted no part of him, even before that night. And as he was confronted by her at the front door, with the knife in his hand, the bloody knife that he removed from the chest of Richard Rockwald, and in the process got splattered with blood from the already dead bodies, he panicked.

He told Sibby he was sorry. But not for killing her family, but because they were dead. He had threatened her father earlier, and now they were all dead, and so he, Brad Kendall, panicked, dropped the knife at her feet, and ran, like a coward . . .and he was still running.

Brad stopped walking. He stopped dead in his tracks. He didn't want to run anymore. He would turn himself in - or let them catch him. Maybe the man back at the restaurant who was looking for him would catch up to him. He wouldn't run anymore; he would stand still until they found him.

Then he could go home - and tell the truth - and see his mother and father - and Sibby, to tell her again how sorry he is and that he's not guilty.

He felt at peace now, and less afraid, as he headed for Browntown. He was halfway there; it wouldn't be long. He quickened his pace.

# Chapter 33

Luther Smith was hungry. He was always hungry, especially after he'd watched people die. Luis Smith had to look at some maps to find out where Steel lived.

They stopped at a Mac Donald's and went inside to eat. They took over a big booth so Luis could spread out the maps of Illinois and McHenry County. Luther ordered three Big Macs, a large order of fries, and a strawberry shake. Luis got a cheeseburger and a small black coffee.

"How you eat all tha' shit and not get fat?" asked Luis.

"I got a good constitution, I guess," said Luther.

"Wha' the fuck you talkin' about?" said Luis.

"I don't know," said Luther. "I'm just hungry."

"This place where this guy, Steel, lives is way the hell out," said Luis.

"Where the fuck is it?" asked Luther.

Parents and children were seated near and every time Luther or Luis used the "F" word, the parents shot a glance in their direction. Luther and Luis were oblivious to the people around them until a young, petite, white mother with two little girls said, "please."

"Sorry, Miss" said Luther, as he gave her his best smile.

She went back to tending her children.

"Let's keep it down," said Luther.

"Fuck her," said Luther.

She heard what he said. She picked up her tray and relocated herself and her two daughters to another table.

"So how far is this place?" asked Luther.

"About two, three hours, if we can find it," said Luis.

"You want to go tonight or wait until tomorrow?" asked Luther.

"I wanted to go today, but it's too damned far," said Luis.

"So, let's go tomorrow," said Luther.

"Okay. Let's go tomorrow morning," said Luis. "What you wanna do tonight?"

"Whatever - get laid, I guess," said Luther.

"My man," said Luis.

# Chapter 34

The night before, after he'd arrived in Browntown, Brad Kendall found all the businesses closed. There weren't many to start with. A Chevron station, a body repair shop, and the Browntown Eatery, all closed. The sign on the restaurant door indicated that it opened at six in the morning and closed at six in the evening.

The Browntown Eatery had ceased doing business for the day about an hour earlier and was locked shut for the night. Brad looked up and down the deserted main road, then wandered behind the restaurant where he discovered a fenced-in area that concealed a green metal Dumpster. He squeezed between the Dumpster and the wall of the building and covered himself with newspapers he'd found piled in the corner.

Now that he'd made up his mind, he hoped they'd find him soon, not even considering how he could turn himself in. He would try to stay warm until morning, when the restaurant opened, but he knew it would be hard, since he was already cold, now that his brisk walk to town had ceased.

As he huddled against the building, covered with his duffel bag  and layers of newspapers, he quickly fell asleep. The hike and his resolution to turn himself in, allowed him to sleep soundly, so soundly, that when he heard the rumble of a garbage pickup truck, he nearly jumped out of his shoes. As he leaped to his feet, the newspapers fell all around him.

His eyes adjusted to a waking state. He looked at his watch. It was almost six A.M. As he reached to open the gate of the fenced-in area to let himself out, someone pulled the gate in the opposite direction. The two startled each other.

"Whoa, what're you doing here?" blurted the trash man.

"Just waiting for the place to open," said Brad.

"Why are you here in the back?" asked the vigilant refuse collector, concerned about his customer, the eatery owner.

"Too cold out front," said Brad. His teeth actually chattered.

The refuse man became less wary. "I can see you're cold," he said. "They should open soon. They're usually early."

"Thanks," said Brad. He stuttered the word.

"By the way," said the collector. "Where's your car?"

"I thumbed my way here," said Brad. "I'm on my way to Dubuque."

"I think I hear them opening up now. They're early today, lucky for you," said the man.

"Thanks," said Brad, as he willed his frozen feet to move forward.

Brad entered the restaurant and realized he was the first customer. A waitress in a pink uniform waved to him. Brad headed to the rear booth, one of six in the place. There were also four tables, while the counter sat six. An older man in a white tee shirt, suspenders, and a white paper hat carried in the morning newspapers. The man reminded Brad of Nick.

The waitress brought a menu but Brad didn't look at it. "Coffee," he said. "And three scrambled eggs, hash browns, and toast."

"Regular or decaf?" she said.

"Regular," he said.

"Can I have the coffee now," he said.

"It's still brewing," she said. "Be just a minute." She was young, like him, but dainty, and pretty, like Sibby.

"You new in town?" she asked.

"Passing through," he said.

"Oh," she said, sounding disappointed.

Other customers wandered in and she left Brad to wait on them. Brad watched her move, efficiently, and with grace. He didn't want to stare so he looked out the window to his right. The sky was dark blue. Soon it would be light. He was glad to be warm again.

Since he hadn't cleaned up after spending the night with the trash, he used the time to refresh himself in the men's room. When he returned to his booth, the waitress greeted him with a coffee pot in each hand.

"Regular, right?" she said.

"Right."

"Where you headed?" she said.

"Iowa."

181

"What's in Iowa?"

"A job - maybe."

"You don't sound too sure," she said.

"I'm not," he said. "I might go back to Illinois."

"Is that where you're from?" she said.

"Yes," he said.

"Why'd you leave?" she said.

"To get away," he said.

"From what?" she asked.

"Stuff," he said.

Customers started arriving at the restaurant with increased frequency. The front door steadily opened and closed. The regulars seated themselves in familiar seats.

"Oops, got to go. Place is filling up."

Minutes later, she brought his order and refilled his coffee mug.

"Anything else?" she said.

"I might have a roll," he said. "you have any?"

"Yes. Fresh every morning," she said. She left to get other orders.

When she took away Brad's dirty plate, she asked, "Decide on that roll?"

"Bring me two," he said.

"Hungry, aren't you?"

He didn't answer. Just nodded his head. He didn't know why, but he felt as if he'd blushed. She poured more coffee.

She returned with the two biggest sweet rolls Brad had ever seen. "Sure you can finish these?" she joked.

"I'll do my best," he said.

"So, did you decide on Iowa or Illinois?" she asked.

"Home to Illinois," he said.

"Good for you," she said.

"Mind if I wait here for my ride?" he said.

"No problem. Who's picking you up, a friend?" she said.

"Sort of," he said.

She poured more coffee, left his bill, and moved to another table.

# Chapter 35

Justin Steel had driven through Monroe after checking out of his motel in Brodhead. He continued to follow Route 11 as he headed west.

A tow truck was hoisting a pickup truck along side the road. Steel recognized it as Nick's by the description he had gotten back at Nick's Restaurant. Steel pulled behind the two trucks that looked like they were mating. A man in a mechanic's jumpsuit was double checking the hoist chain.

Steel approached the tow truck driver and asked, "where are you taking it?"

"Who're you?" he asked.

"Name's Steel." He gave the man his business card.

The man looked at Steel, then the card, then back at Steel. He scratched his head, then replied, "I'm takin' it over to Brodhead."

"Police look at it yet?" asked Steel.

"They just left a minute or two ago," he said.

"Where are you taking it in Brodhead?" asked Steel.

"Place called Nick's Restaurant," said the tow truck man. "By the way, who's payin' for the tow?"

"Who hired you?" asked Steel.

"Police called me."

"I'm sure Nick will pay you," said Steel.

"If you say so," said the man.

The driver got in his truck, made a U turn and headed in the direction Steel just came from. The back end of Nick's truck was up in the air as the truck rolled on its two front tires, the ones without the flat. Steel didn't know if this was the right method for towing but he figured the driver must know his business. As the driver and the truck passed Steel, he saw the name on the door, Browntown Garage.

Steel drove his car to Browntown, a two minute drive. All the while, he surveyed both sides of the road looking for telltale signs, but he saw none that said, "this way to Brad Kendall." Steel hoped he hadn't lost him.

Steel stopped at the Chevron Service Station, and pumped his own gas. So much for service. He asked the clerk inside about Brad Kendall as he flashed his photo. She said she never saw him and went back to reading her magazine.

Steel saw the Browntown Garage, repairs and towing, about a block up the road. He decided there would be nothing there.

Not expecting much, he thought he'd try the Browntown Eatery. Most likely, no one saw Brad. For all he knew, Brad could be hundreds of miles away by now.

He could have hitched a ride or stolen another vehicle, one that hadn't yet been reported.

Steel walked in and approached the cash register. An old man in a tee shirt and white hat sat on a stool with his one foot on a rung and his other foot touching the floor. When Steel showed him the head shot of Brad, the man shook his head. He hadn't seen him. He went back to his sitting.

A petite waitress offered to seat him, but Steel declined. He flashed Brad's picture and told her what he'd told the others, that his hair is longer now and he may have a beard. Nick had described him to Steel. It was possible the beard could be shaved off.

She took the pencil from behind her ear, and as she looked up to Steel's face, with a nod of her head, while pointing with the pencil, she gestured toward the far end of the eating area.

"I think he's waiting for you," she said.

"Is he?" said Steel, as he spotted the large bearded boy in the booth drinking coffee.

"You're here to take him to Illinois, aren't you?" she said.

Steel didn't answer, though he wondered why she knew so much. His hand went under his coat to his shoulder holster. He'd put it back on at the motel once he found out his quarry was near. Cautiously, he approached Kendall's booth.

Brad recognized Steel as the man he'd seen at Nick's Restaurant the day before. Steel couldn't believe the boy was smiling at him. Kendall was glad to see the man who had come to capture him.

"Put your hands on the table where I can see them," said Steel, just loud enough for Brad to hear.

The smile disappeared from Brad's face as he complied.

"Stand up and move away from the table, son. I'm going to pat you down. Are you carrying?"

Brad got up, not fully understanding the man's concern.

Briskly, Steel turned him and frisked him. He was amazed at the size of him and of the firmness of his muscles. Steel found no weapons. Customers stopped momentarily to observe, then went back to their food.

Steel moved Brad's duffel bag to his side of the booth and motioned for the boy to sit back down and to keep his hands on the table. Steel was glad the boy didn't put up a tussle. He would have been a test of strength; youth against age, novice against professional, power against power.

"I've been waiting for you," said Brad.

"You have? Why?," said Steel.

"You're here to take me back, aren't you?"

"Yes," said Steel.

"Can I finish my roll?" said Brad.

"I suppose," said Steel. He had been ready for confrontation from the would-be killer. At least, some resistance. But nothing. Just conversation over breakfast.

"My name is Steel."

"Hello, Mr. Steel."

"Just Steel."

"Okay," he said, as he kept munching his roll.

# Chapter 36

Luis and Luther parked their car in front of the gate that blocked their entry to the residence of Justin Steel. Because of Donofrio's connections, they learned that Steel was Marshall Brisby.

"Is this the place where Brisby lives?" asked Luther.

"Looks like it," said Luis.

"Are you sure?" asked Luther.

"How the fuck do I know," said Luis. "I say it looks like it."

"Okay, okay, calm down," said Luther.

"Let's leave the car to the side of the road," said Luis. "Then we walk around someplace there is a hole in the fence and then we go in."

"Are you sure this is the place?" said Luther again.

"Shut up," said Luis. "Follow me."

They followed the fence line for about a block. In places the fence was wrought iron and in others it was wire mesh, but always it was topped with barbed wire. The metallic barrier angled and disappeared into heavy brush. Luis and Luther made their way through thistles, dry vines, and tree roots that grew out of the ground. Ultimately, they came across what they were looking for, a tree limb extended over the barbed fence.

They struggled as they climbed the tree, then crawled slowly over the protruding limb. Once past the barbs, they dropped eight feet to the ground, now on the other side of the obstruction. It was light out, but it was difficult to see in the heavily wooded confine.

"We're in," said Luis.

"This better be the place," said Luther. "Which way now?"

"Follow me," said Luis.

The Hessmullers were instructed to let Scrap Iron systematically roam the grounds four times a day. It was time for the dog's second run, the first having been done at daybreak. Almost nine, they sent the dog out again. If he didn't return in fifteen minutes, the Hessmullers were instructed to call the police. Steel had arranged for their swift response in an emergency or potential danger.

Luis and Luther had wheedled their way toward the house and were about a hundred yards away when they saw the dog get released. They stayed low in the brush but the dog ran directly for them, silent and swift.

Once the Hessmullers let the dog out, they closed the door and went about their business within the house.

Having done this task so many times before, they stopped being cautious.

Had not Luther and Luis spotted the dog immediately, they would have been caught completely by surprise. But they had time to prepare.

"Oh, shit," said Luther. "What the fuck we gonna do now?"

"We shoot the mutha-fucker between the eyes," said Luis. "We wait 'til he get closer."

Ten feet away, Scrap Iron stopped, stared at his prey, and issued a menacing growl. Luis and Luther didn't move. The dog crept closer, continuing his growl.

Luis aimed at Scrap Iron and fired. Were it not for the dog's remarkable agility and speed, it would have caught the slug. Instead, it ran until it was out of their vision.

"Ha, ha," laughed Luis. "Fuckin' coward dog."

"The dog's a woos," said Luther. "C'mon, let's go."

The two men walked boldly to the front door of the house and pounded on the front door. Before Gus or Emily could stop her, Sibby opened the door and Mex and Thumbs pushed their way in.

Scrap Iron laid in the high grass and watched the proceedings from a safe distance, but crept closer and closer to the house. The dog had behaved as Steel had trained him - to run from gunfire. Steel had lost the first Scrap Iron to a bullet. He wanted to make sure this one would be cautious enough to stay alive. The dog did as he was taught, nothing more, nothing less. And still, he crept closer.

# Chapter 37

Steel cuffed Brad Kendall to the inside of the car while he went inside to call Mike Collins. Steel didn't expect Brad to run, but he didn't want to chance it. He told Brad he had no choice and Brad said he understood even though his huge wrists chafed under the metal restraints.

"Hello Mike," said Steel. "I've got him."

"You have who? Kendall? You have Kendall? Where?" said an excited Mike Collins.

"We're in a burb called Browntown, in Wisconsin, not too far from Brodhead," said Steel.

"How in the hell did you find him?" said Mike.

"Actually, he found me," said Steel. "More or less."

"Did he give you much trouble? Did you have help? Tell me," said Mike.

"No trouble," said Steel. "We chatted over coffee and now we're coming in"

"You always make everything sound easy," said Mike.

"This time it was. I'll tell you the rest when we come in," said Steel.

"I'll want to talk to him the minute you bring him in . . . before anybody else," said Mike.

"Fair enough," said Steel.

"Did he say anything yet? About the killing?" said Mike.

"Not yet. He just wants to come home."

"Will you be all right alone with him?" asked Mike.

"No, I need you to hold my hand," said Steel.

"Okay. I asked for that. See you when you get here."

Steel picked up two coffees for the trip home to Illinois. He didn't want to stop along the way. As he approached the car, he saw Brad wasn't in the vehicle anymore. The loose cuffs dangled from the steering wheel. Steel placed the coffee cups on the hood and was prepared to pursue his prey again.

"Over here, Mr. Steel," hollered Brad.

He was sitting on a tree stump about thirty feet from the automobile. He stood up and approached Steel. Steel had his hand inside his coat and on his concealed revolver.

"The cuffs hurt my wrists, so I took them off. Is that okay?" Brad slipped into the front passenger seat. "Are we ready to go?"

Steel released the grip on his holster, shook his head and chuckled, "We're ready." He removed the cups of coffee from the hood and placed them between himself and Brad.

"Do we have to put the cuffs back on?" said Brad.

194

"No. I guess not," said Steel. "Doesn't look like they'd do any good anyway, does it?"

"I thought maybe you had some better ones," said Brad.

"That was my best pair," Steel said. He marvelled at the boy's strength.

"Sorry, I broke them," he said.

"I can buy more," said Steel.

"Can I offer to pay for them?" said Brad.

Steel didn't answer. He wasn't sure if Brad was putting him on or if he was for real. He suspected he was for real - but was he a killer?

# Chapter 38

Mex and Thumbs were inside the house now. As Sibby backed away, Luis walked toward her, while Luther double-bolted the door.

"Watch her," said Luis, meaning Sibby. He ran to the kitchen and knocked the phone from Emily's hand before she could dial. Gus charged Luis but the old man was no match for Luis who pushed him aside and butted him in the head with his pistol as the old man whizzed past him.

Gus tumbled to the floor and stayed there. His hands were spread above his head as he laid face down, his head turned to one side. Blood trickled from the back of his head, where Luis had struck him.

"Oh my God. You've killed him," cried Emily. "You've killed him." She tried to go to her husband's aid but Luis grabbed her by the hair and half dragged her to Luther.

"Here, watch her, too. Do I gotta do everythin' myself?" said Luis.

Luther shrugged as he held onto Sibby and Emily.

Luis darted in and out of rooms, his aimed revolver leading the way. After a few minutes, he seemed satisfied no one else was in the house.

Emily kept trying to get away from Luther but he held her easily across her shoulders with his left arm. Emily didn't notice Luther's missing thumb. All she could think of was her injured, perhaps dead, husband lying on the cold floor.

Sibby, though younger and stronger than Emily, didn't struggle. She whimpered in Luther's strong right-armed hold.

"My arms are getting tired," said Luther. "Can I let them go?"

"Listen up, you two bitches. If the man let's you go, are you gonna behave? Are you gonna sit down nice?" said Luis.

Sibby nodded in acquiescence. Emily stared with contempt at the Mexican hoodlum in front of her. Luis averted his eyes.

"Okay. Sit'em down," said Luis.

Luther threw Sibby onto the sofa. She lay where he put her and continued to whimper. He flung Emily into the side chair, but she rebounded immediately and sat upright, and perched on the edge of the chair, as if ready to spring.

Her man was down; her husband, her Gus. She looked first at Gus, then Luis, then Gus, back and forth. She stopped and stared only at Luis, with hatred.

Luis threw his hands up in the air. "You want a piece of me, bitch?" he said.

She sprang to her feet and attacked him. Luther laughed. Luis pushed her off easily and slapped her across the face with the back of his hand.

"What you have to do that for? She's an old lady," said Luther.

"She's a fuckin' ol' lady bitch, is what she is. An' soon she gonna be a dead ol' lady bitch," said Luis.

Luther shrugged his shoulders. He couldn't argue with that kind of logic.

"So where's Steel?" asked Luis.

Emily didn't answer. She acted as if she hadn't heard the question. Luther grabbed the hair on the back of her head and turned her face to within inches of his face. He pointed his gun at her husband lying on the floor in the open kitchen and said to her face, "Do you wanna see me kill your man, if he ain't dead already?" He sprayed spittle as he spoke. Her right eye that was starting to swell shut, popped open, when he issued his threat. She shook her head.

"Again, I ask you. Where is Steel?" said Luis, as he continued to hold her by the hair.

Again, Emily shook her head.

Luis was about to strike her once more.

"Wait," blurted Sibby from the sofa. "I'll tell you."

Luis motioned Luther to Emily. They traded sentry positions as Luis went to Sibby.

"So tell me," said Luis.

"He's not here," she said.

"I know that, you stupid bitch," said Luis, as he raised his hand to strike her.

She covered her face with both hands. "He calls in. We don't know where he is at this moment, but he calls in."

"When?" he asked.

"Whenever he wants."

"I got this number from your uncle and auntie. How come Steel don't answer?"

Sibby recognized the piece of paper with Steel's private phone number on it. "They wouldn't give you that number unless you made them."

"No, they jus' said, here Luis, take this number if you want to call Steel."

"You're a liar," said Sibby.

Luis grinned.

"You right. I kill them an' I can kill you, too, if you don' tell me how I can call Steel."

Sibby couldn't believe what she had just heard. Yet, she knew she must believe this man who stood before her, menacing her.

"You killed Uncle Frank?"

"Un huh. An' you auntie, too."

With suddenness, it became very quiet. Two frightened women, scared to death. Two men, with guns, Smith and Smith, had reached an impasse.

They could kill the women and leave but they still wouldn't have Steel, or Brisby, or whoever he was. And it was him they came for. "Call the number, again," said Luther.

# Chapter 39

Steel had decided to take Route 69 south from Monroe to Freeport, Illinois and connect with Route 20. They could proceed from there to Rockford and access the toll road to Chicago. Steel wanted the speediest route, while Brad seemed to be enjoying the ride.

Steel didn't appear to be worried about his passenger anymore. Brad certainly was strong enough to overpower him but if he was going to try anything, he would have done so by now.

"Where are we?" asked Brad, who had been quiet until now.

"Halfway between Freeport and Rockford," said Steel.

"How much longer until we get to where we're going?" asked Brad.

"About two hours," said Steel. He couldn't help thinking that Brad's question was like a little boy's question. Only a few years difference.

"You don't have to answer me," said Steel. "But did you kill those people?"

"I don't mind answering you, sir," said Brad. "No, I didn't kill those people, as you call them." He turned his head away, then looked straight ahead. Out of the corner of his eye, Steel could see tears forming in Brad's eyes, tears that he tried to blink away.

"Those people," Brad continued, "are - were Sibby's parents. I baby-sat Richie and Cindy. We played games together."

"Why did you run?"

"I don't know. Scared, I guess. I felt guilty."

"Why did you feel guilty?"

"Because I told Sibby I wished her parents were dead . . . and then they were."

"And you didn't kill them?"

"I swear to God, sir. I didn't kill them."

"Then you shouldn't feel guilty," said Steel.

"I still feel responsible," said Brad.

"If you didn't kill them, how did the bloody weapon end up in your hand?"

"I pulled it out of Mr. Rockwald's chest." Brad blanched as he recalled the act.

"What were you doing in the house that night?"

"I came to talk to Mr. and Mrs. Rockwald, to plead with them about breaking me and Sibby up."

"Maybe Sibby wanted to break up," said Steel.

"I've thought about that a lot the past month," said Brad.

"Any conclusions," said Steel.

"None, sir."

"So, what did you do? Break in while they were sleeping?"

"No, sir. The front door was open and some of the lights in the house were on. I called out, but nobody answered. I hollered, loud. Then I got mad why they didn't answer me. I thought they were toying with me or being cruel. I was real mad, you see. So, I charged into their bedroom . . . and there they were.

"I stood and stared at them but then it dawned on me that I should do something. I guess that's when I pulled out the knife. I checked on Richie and Cindy. They were dead, too. I'd never seen anybody dead before but I could see they were dead, all of them."

"How long were you in the house?"

"I don't know. Seems like forever. I never saw so much blood in my life. I still have nightmares."

"I can imagine," said Steel. Nightmares were something both had in common.

"Why did you run?"

"I didn't plan to run away. I heard somebody in the house. I thought it came from the back but it must have been the front, because when I got there, I saw it was Sibby. I didn't want her to see what I saw. I realized I still had the bloody knife in my hand. I dropped it.

"I told Sibby I was sorry and I tried to comfort her but she was afraid of me. She might have thought I did it. I think she did think that. I wanted to run away . . . and I guess I did, didn't I?"

"Yes, you did," said Steel.

"I'm sorry for all the trouble I caused," said Brad. "Sibby must hate me."

"Yes, she does." Steel didn't attempt a lie.

"Oh, God," he said.

"Your parents asked me to find you, to bring you home safely," said Steel. "They believe you . . . they love you." Steel almost couldn't get the words out. The uttering was laced with emotion as if he had spoken in the parents' voice.

"Thank God," said Brad. He seemed to be running out of words.

Rockford, two miles, was the sign they passed. At that juncture, Steel's phone rang.

"Steel," he answered. He hadn't received a call for some time. He realized he was again within the calling area.

"Mr. Steel?" said Luis. "How nice."

"Who is this?" asked Steel.

"An ol', ol', friend, Mr. Steel."

"If you were an old friend, you wouldn't call me mister."

"Tha's right." Luis drawled it out. "You are Steel. Ha! Ha! Like man of steel?" chuckled Luis.

"Close enough," said Steel. "Who is this. Answer, or I'll hang up."

"Don' do that, Steel. I got some friends of yours here. An ol' lady an' a ol' man, an' a sweet fresh muchacha, an' a scared shit less dog. Come home, Steel. Don' call the cops or everybody dies. All I wan' is you, Steel. Some unfinished business from a long time ago, Steel - or should I call you, Brisby?" The connection broke.

Is everything okay, sir?" Brad saw Steel's knuckles whiten as he gripped the steering wheel.

"We have to stop at my house," said Steel, as he floored the accelerator.

204

# Chapter 40

Steel knew when to speed up and when to slow down. He didn't want to attract the attention of the police. Calling the police for assistance was not an option. The man on the phone said to come alone and his voice sounded eerily familiar.

Emily, Gus, and Sibby were in danger and if he couldn't save them, how could he justify his existence to himself. His whole reason for being was to help others. But not like a lawyer, not like a priest; not even like an accountant. His role was different but precise. It was to rescue the innocent from evil; to avenge the aggrieved; to vanquish the aggressors. He was Steel, Justin Steel, a name, a man he created, who was strong, where Marshall Brisby was weak. Steel sought justice, whereas Brisby hid behind peace.

He alone had placed the people closest to him, Gus and Emily, in peril. He had not taken Sibby to a sanctuary, but to a battlefield of danger.

Marshall Brisby had let his family die, Genevieve, his wife, and Crispin and Martin, his sons. He might as well have done the killing himself. Excuses were not acceptable and regrets only led to damnation. He could have died himself, he knew, and perhaps should have.

Yet, he lived, to try and make up for his shortcomings, to try to make right what could never be made right. He would try to save others as he could not save his family, as he could not save himself.

As they drove, Steel informed Brad of the danger Sibby and the others were in. Brad feared for Sibby, the girl, no, the woman he loved, no matter what she felt for him. He too had misgivings over what might have been had he arrived early enough to save the Rochwalds from their grizzly death. He couldn't take back the venomous words he spoke to Sibby, of how he wished her parents dead. All he could do is repeat how sorry he was and, if she let him, how much he still loved her.

Two men, hell bent with purpose, drove furiously to right a wrong, to save who they cared for, no matter what harm would come to themselves in the process. They had to intervene in the race between time and death.

Steel entered the road that would bring him to his property. Within a block of the gate, he stopped the car, took a deep breath, checked his shoulder holster and the weapon in it. He discarded his tie, his ring, and all other nuisances.

"This will be dangerous," said Steel. "You should stay in the car."

"Like hell," said Brad. "I'm going in with you."

"The man, and whoever else may be with him, may be trained killers. I'm almost sure of it. I think I recognized his voice."

"I'm still going in," Brad started to get out of the car. Steel grabbed his sleeve and held him back.

"Wait," said Steel "Let's devise a plan." Steel realized he couldn't stop him and perhaps he could use him. But could he keep him safe?

"Have you ever fired a gun?" asked Steel.

"No, sir."

"Cut the sir. No time for that. Just say yes or no, and call me Steel. Just Steel.

"What would you do if someone came at you with a knife or a switchblade?" said Steel.

Brad pondered the question. "I'd let him cut me, then I'd take the blade and make him eat it." Steel had to smile; he believed Brad would.

"What would you do with a bullet? Stop it with your teeth?"

"If I could, I would," said Brad. "I'd risk being shot if it meant saving Sibby . . . and your friends."

"Okay, be quiet," said Steel. "I'm going to call. I don't think anyone inside knows you're with me."

Steel's call to his home was picked up on the third ring. No one spoke.

"Hello," said Steel. "I'm almost home."

"Where the fuck are you?" said Luis.

"About fifteen minutes away," Steel lied.

"You got ten minutes," said Luis. "Or they all die."

"If I speed, I may be stopped," said Steel. "I'm trying not to bring attention to myself."

"Hokay, but hurry-up."

"I'm coming," said Steel. "Don't hurt anyone."

Luis hung up the phone. He had the Gringo by the short hairs. He liked being in charge. Mister Smith. The Boss.

"Listen up," Steel said to Brad. "I'm going in the front. They'll be looking for me. They don't know about you. Here's the key to the back of the house. Come in through the back porch."

"Okay," said Brad, and he started to get out of the car again.

"Wait, I'm not finished. We'll drive in together. Halfway in, I'll let you get out and you have to stay out of sight."

Brad nodded. He understood.

"Take this gun," said Steel. "Put it in your jacket pocket. Zip it in so it won't fall out. They'll pat me down so I can't be carrying."

Brad handled the weapon as if it was leprosy or as if it were covered with molasses. There was no doubt in Steel's mind that Brad was not accustomed to firearms.

"My dog may be out there or he may be in the house. He may already have been shot or killed or he may have gotten away. I don't know. If I trained him right, he's still out there."

"I'm not afraid of dogs," said Brad.

"He's not just any dog," said Steel. "If he sees you and he doesn't know you, he could hurt you, or even kill you."

"So what do I do?" said Brad.

"Disarm him . . . with words. His name is Scrap Iron. Call him to you and say, 'debits and credits.' Got that?" said Steel.

"Scrap Iron . . .debits and credits . . .right," said Brad, thinking of how weird the command language was.

"Once I'm in the house I should be able to hold everyone's attention. That's when you come in the back way. If the dog finds you, after you say the command words, he'll follow you. You don't have to say anything else. Let him in the house. He knows his job. Just don't get in his way."

"Must be some kind of dog," said Brad.

Steel didn't respond to Brad's comment. Instead, he advocated caution.

"Don't be a hero. Just get in the house, bring the gun, and follow my lead."

"I don't care what happens to me," said Brad. "As long as Sibby is okay."

"You're mother and father care," said Steel. "What do I tell them if you're dead?"

Brad pondered this. "I'll be all right," he said.

"I promised your parents I'd bring you home safely," said Steel. "Let's all get out of this alive. This is serious business."

"Good plan," said Brad. "I agree." He was wound tight, like a middle linebacker ready to charge the backfield, as he did on the University of Chicago football team.

"God help us," Steel said aloud, and he meant it. Situations like this brought his religious inclinations to a crescendo. "We have only a few minutes, so hurry, and be careful. Remember, debits and credits."

209

"Debits and credits," said Brad. He slipped out of the car and for a man his size moved with incredible precision and grace. Dry grass and brush swiftly concealed him.

Steel waited in the car, hidden from view where he parked it. He knew the blind spot. He knew what he himself couldn't see from the house when he looked out. Brad needed a head start. Running low, sometimes crawling, he needed time.

Brad was now alongside the house, about two hundred feet from it. He needed to maneuver himself to the rear. Twigs snapped, leaves crackled. His jeans were wet from crawling in the frozen and damp underbrush. Almost there, he thought.

The growl came first, then he saw the dog. Silent, like him, it had caught him unaware.

"Oh shit," he said. The dog was huge. "Nice doggy," he stuttered. "Good dog. Good iron dog." He couldn't remember what to say. The dog boldly crept toward him. "Good Scrap Iron," he remembered. "Kibbles and Bits." No, that's not it, he thought. "Good dog," he started again. "Good Scrap Iron . . . debits and credits." Thank God, he remembered. He repeated, "Good Scrap Iron, debits and credits."

The dog came and licked his face. Both were on all fours, both bulked with muscle, bound together, inextricably friends. "Debits and credits." He patted the dog's head. Scrap Iron followed his lead as he continued to make his way to the back of the house.

Justin Steel drove up to the front of the house where he could be easily seen. He got out of his Taurus slowly and approached the front of his house and knocked on the front door. Between the house and the car, he could have been shot. He doubted that was how he was supposed to die. He was wanted inside. He had no choice but to gamble.

A big black man who looked familiar opened the door and backed away. He held a revolver in his right hand and aimed it at Steel. His left hand held Emily as a shield in front of him.

The sight of the missing thumb on the black man's left hand flashed Steel's nightmares into reality. The thumb less left hand was the same hand that restrained him that night, long ago, when he desperately struggled to free himself, but could not. His pathetic weakness permitted his wife and children to be savagely murdered, then burned in the house fire, as he escaped, alive.

The black man looked as formidable as ever. He wouldn't be easy to take down. Steel began to doubt his own resolve, his ability to fight and cope. Would his training be enough or was it all for nothing? Steel forced himself to be cool.

"What do you want and why are you in my house?" said Steel.

The Mexican who held Sibby as his shield stepped from the darkness of the hallway like a serpent from a crevice in the earth.

"I'll ask the questions, Gringo," said Luis. "But first, we check you out. Search him," he said to Luther, as he took Emily from him. "No funny stuff, Gringo, or the bitches die."

"No funny stuff," said Steel.

Luther patted Steel down, found the empty shoulder holster, but nothing else. "Where's your weapon?" demanded Luther.

"I dumped it before I came in. I didn't think you'd let me keep it, anyway," said Steel.

"He's not armed," said Luther.

"Here, take these bitches." Luis handed Emily and Sibby to Luther. He wrapped an arm around each woman and was still able to hold his pistol in his right hand.

Luis waved his revolver at Steel, keeping a safe distance of ten feet. Steel didn't move. Instead he surveyed the room and planned his next moves, if he had any coming.

"I know you, Gringo," said Luis. "You're fuckin' Brisby, Marshall, fuckin', Brisby, the accountant. What you do with your sexy pajamas, like you wore that night? They was so cute." Luis laughed at the recollection.

Steel also recognized his opponent. The unforgettable scar spanned his throat. At last, he had the two men who killed his family . . . or they had him.

"You a fuckin' woos, Brisby," said Luis.

"The name is Steel."

"Oh, 'scuse me Mister Steel."

"Not mister, just Steel."

"Ooh, I'm shakin'. Steel, ooh," Luis mocked.

Steel would not allow himself to be intimidated. He waited all these years - trained all these years - all these long years - for vengeance. He was hard now. He wasn't Brisby, he was Steel. He wasn't just pretending, he was Steel. He had crossed over.

"Brisby, Steel, what the fuck's the difference. You gonna die, Gringo."

212

Luther held the two women like rag dolls. He chuckled sadistically. He was having a good time.

Steel heard the back door open and close. No one else was aware that Brad had entered. Only Steel was expecting him.

Steel also surmised that his best bet might be to feign cowardice. He was not above it. Perhaps this time it could work in his favor. Whatever it took to save, Emily, Sibby, and Gus. He realized he hadn't seen Gus. He didn't know if he should speak his name. Perhaps he was hiding. It was a chance Steel decided to take.

"Where's Gus," asked Steel.

"The ol' man's sleepin'," said Luis, as he gestured to the kitchen floor where Gus lay unconscious or dead.

"Is he alive?" asked Steel.

"Who the fuck cares?" said Luis. "You all be dead soon."

Only Steel saw Scrap Iron laying low in the corner in the darkness awaiting his master's command. While the dog was trained to run from gunfire, Steel could override that training with the command, "deadbeat," which would instruct the dog to attack the gunman. Only the command, "profit," would stop the dog from tearing the gunman to shreds and killing him. Steel waited for the chance.

"Look," said Steel. "I'm sorry if I made you angry. Please don't hurt me. Do what you want with the others, just don't hurt me."

"No balls, " said Luis. "Woos."

"Please," said Steel. "I don't even know how to address you. What should I call you?"

Luis liked this new respect. "Mr. Smith," said Luis.

"Mr. Smith, I know you killed my wife and children. But that was a long time ago. I've already forgotten. Did you kill the Rochwalds, too. I'll bet you did. I didn't know them; it doesn't bother me. I'll bet you're not afraid of anyone."

Luis was starting to like the kiss-ass. At least he knew how to give respect. It didn't matter. He would kill him like he killed everybody else. "Yeah, sure," said Luis. "He owed Mr. Donofrio money." As soon as he'd said it, he wished he hadn't referred to him as mister, but it was too late. "I took out the whole family. I'm too smart to leave witnesses."

Luther had his hands over Emily's and Sibby's mouths now, just like he did those many years ago when he held a helpless Marshall Brisby. The women couldn't speak but Steel could see questions in their eyes.

"How did you get in, through the window?" said Steel.

"No windows for me. I come in the front door and go out the back door," he lied. "That dumb kid come in the front door and took the fall, the big ass hole."

Like a big blur, though not cued by Steel, but rather by his own over-sensitivity, Brad streaked across the room from behind and jumped the arrogant Mexican. Steel was forced to act quickly.

"Scrap Iron, 'deadbeat'." This wasn't the way Steel had it planned. Brad's impetuousness forced his move.

Scrap Iron raced for Luther and crunched his gun hand so hard bones cracked. Luther shrieked in pain. With his immense strength, he slammed the dog into the wall. Scrap Iron fell into a heap. But Emily and Sibby got away from Luther's grip.

Brad's superior size and strength knocked Luis to the floor as they both went down in a thud. Brad was about to smash his fist into Mex's face when Mex shot him. Brad groaned and fell into a lump.

Steel had to act quickly. He kicked the gun from Luis' hand, causing it to skitter across the room. The Mexican produced a switchblade almost instantly and poised himself in a slashing mode.

"C'mon, Gringo woos," he taunted Steel.

Steel had no time to play with him. He had to get to Sibby and Emily before Luther recovered. Steel feigned a move, Mex slashed, and Steel grabbed his wrist, snapping it with one motion. The switchblade fell to the floor. Steel kicked it away. Though in pain, Mex got up, so Steel punched him in the mouth, sending the squat assassin flailing backwards.

Steel turned his attention to the big black man, who was reaching for the pistol that lay on the floor. He tried to grab it with his thumb less left hand. Steel punched him straight across the mouth. The black man took the blow smiling, as blood inside his mouth leaked through his gapped front teeth. He spit blood between the teeth and went for the gun again.

Steel stepped on his hand but the man continued to grip the pistol. The gun went off. Without aiming, he managed to shoot Sibby. God, Steel thought, everyone's going to die.

He could not dawdle with this man. He must kill him. Steel shot his hand out in an away motion and caught the man's Adam's apple, causing him to gurgle and gasp for air. While he was preoccupied in trying not to suffocate, Steel deftly swung behind the behemoth. He grasped the man's head in both hands and jerked it.

He heard the crack and the man fell to the floor, eyes wide open, staring but not seeing.

Steel returned to Mex who had regained consciousness and held the previously discarded gun in his hand. Steel could not, would not stop. With all the dexterity and swiftness he possessed, Steel dodged and weaved his way toward Mex in hopes of overtaking him.

Steel realized he had made a mistake when he felt the bullet enter his shoulder. He felt as if he'd slammed into a brick wall. The pain was searing; it burned, like fire.

Scrap Iron was recovering from his headlong crash into the wall. The 'deadbeat' command was still in effect. He raced for the Mexican named Smith. Mex fired, striking the dog midair. My God, thought Steel, we really are all going to die.

Scrap Iron's lunge purchased time for Steel to recoup. He rushed the desperate killer. When he made contact with Mex, the gun became dislodged. Steel experienced excruciating pain from his bullet wound.

Steel couldn't think of himself. The carnage caused and the pain inflicted by this man's hand was far more excruciating and horrible than Steel's wound. Luis Smith and his cohort had ravaged Sibby's family and now Sibby. Brad and Gus and he himself were part of the toll. Even Scrap Iron was not spared.

Worst of all, this man had killed his Genevieve and his twin sons. There could be no forgiveness for this. No respite. No salvation. Steel knew what he should do; what he must do. All the rage caused by the deaths and suffering focused in Steel's right arm as he grabbed Mex by the neck and lifted him off the floor. Steel could feel the long scar that was on the man's neck.

Luis Smith's arms and legs flailed, but to no avail. Steel's strength and resolve were too powerful. Mex's eyes bulged and his tongue hung out. A gurgling sound emanated from the dying man's throat.

Steel could hold him no longer nor could he bear to watch. In one swift movement, He crushed Luis' skull to the floor. Blood leaked onto the carpet and Mex was no more.

Steel laid prostrate on the carpet next to him, exhausted, physically and emotionally. He cried out loud like a lunatic with pain.

Emily alone remained standing. She dialed the phone and made her call. She then knelt beside Gus, finally able to cry.

The ambulance and police would arrive soon.

# Epilogue

Seven months have passed since that night when some people died and some would begin their lives. Luis Smith and Luther Smith, the odd couple were dead; Mex and Thumbs ceased to exist.

Sibby Rockwald had survived, physically, at least. Her ordeal would never be over. She had taken a bullet in her left thigh. A scar would remain but the pain would eventually be forgotten. The emotional scars would haunt her waking hours and her sleeping dreams until her life's end. At least, she knew that Brad had not killed her family. She hugged him when she left to go to Southern Cal. Steel helped with her tuition. But she and Brad knew they could never be together.

Brad had rescued Sibby. He knew as did she, that in time, most of his pain would cease. Brad had been gut shot and his initial suffering was severe as was his blood loss. But he was young and strong and in excellent physical condition. After a while, Brad's parents forgave Steel for allowing their boy to be hurt. Especially, when Brad insisted it was his own fault. His football playing days were over but he continued his education at the University of Chicago, greatly due to Steel's financial contribution.

Steel had never intended to put Gus and Emily into danger and he wouldn't have been surprised if they both walked. But they stayed. Gus had had a concussion but he recovered fully. That's all Emily wanted, her man.

Steel offered them money or a new house and they were offended by the offer. To just remain in his employ was what they wanted. They thought of Steel as a son. He, in turn, thought of them as parents, the only family he now had.

Scrap Iron gave everybody a scare but he pulled through. He'd never be the dog he once was, but he'd always be Steel's friend. Steel would train another dog to help Scrap Iron patrol the premises.

Mike Collins came to the hospital the night they all were rushed in. Mike stayed with everyone for days until he was certain they would all pull through. He saw to Scrap Iron's care as well. He was sure Steel would have wanted it that way.

Mike told Steel that the FBI didn't arrest anyone in their money laundering investigation. Donofrio was the last link and he left the country. No one's even looking for him.

All the Rockwald's assets were sold. There was just enough to cover the liabilities. What happened to the money Richard Rockwald stashed was a mystery. It may be sitting in some overseas account waiting to be claimed, but no one knows where.

Justin Steel is trying to resume a life of some normalcy, having recently recovered from his gunshot injury. His emotional wounds are also healing. His nightmares are less frequent. More pleasant dreams of Genevieve and the twins occupy his sleeping hours. He dreams of them in a happy place.

Marshall Brisby is beginning to reemerge. He sleeps later each morning. He has his music and reading. There is also the satisfaction of helping Sibby and Brad, who he thinks of as daughter and son, or at least, niece and nephew.

Everybody lived; nobody died, except those who were supposed to. That's something. Luis Smith and Luther Smith have gone to hell, where they belong. Goodness and justice have triumphed.

Steel and Scrap Iron still run each morning, but not as long or as fast as they once did. A more leisurely run, more affection for the dog he almost lost, more savoring of what he has gained, and less lamenting over what he has lost; this is his new life.

One thought haunts him. Was Donofrio the man behind Luis Smith and Luther Smith? If so, not all business is finished. Perhaps he and Donofrio will cross paths and the final chapter will be written. Until then, life is good.

# Quick & Easy
# Order Form

---

By mail: Send order and make check payable to Chris Mystery Publishing. P.O.Box 471, Harvard, Illinois 60033.

Please send _____ copies of **One More Time**. *$12.95 each*

Please send _____ copies of **Just Steel**. *$12.95 each*

If you are not satisfied, simply return the unused books for a full refund.

Ship to:

Name_____

Address _____

City_____ State_____ Zip_____

Telephone_____

e-mail_____

Sales tax. Please add 6.25% for an Illinois address.

Shipping. Please add $1.00 for each book ordered.

Please pay by check or money order.

Chris Mystery Publishing, P.O.Box 471, Harvard, IL 60033
e-mail chrismys@mc.net

# ONE MORE TIME
## *by*
## *Ed Orszula*

Pete Fletcher is in a coma and near death. His family and friends keep vigil near his hospital bed. Pete's mind goes through its own private torment as he anticipates his life flashing before him. He strives to change the life he had lived to one he would have preferred and in the process, two lives, side by side, appear to him. There is plenty of baseball action as the unlikely Cubs are led to new heights by the legendary Pete Fletcher, quite possibly the greatest player ever. His high school coach, Harry Milhouse, later becomes the manager of the Cubs. As his friend, he plays a major role in Pete's development as a player and person as Pete strives to overcome the stigma of alcoholism and adultery. Pete and Will Turner, his childhood friend and later his nemesis, battle for the love of Aggie Fairchild. Pete soon discovers that baseball fame is meaningless without Aggie beside him. Pete chooses on his deathbed to become the greatest baseball player in history and to have the love of Aggie. But did he choose too much and what is he willing to give up to ensure his survival as he lives his life ...one more time?

Check out your favorite bookstore or use the quick and easy order form.

Printed by Morris Publishing
3212 E. Hwy 30
Kearney, NE  68847
1-800-650-7888